FOUR MONEY

EVER AND ALWAYS DUET, BOOK 1

JAYNE RYLON

HAPPY ENDINGS PUBLISHING

Copyright © 2020 by Jayne Rylon

All rights reserved.

No part of this book may be reproduced or shared in any form or by any electronic or mechanical means—including email, file-sharing groups, and peer-to-peer programs—without written permission from the author, except for the use of brief quotations in a book review.

If you have purchased a copy of this ebook, thank you. I greatly appreciate knowing you would never illegally share your copy of this book. This is the polite way of me saying don't be a thieving asshole, please and thank you!

If you're reading this book and did not purchase it, or it was not purchased for your use only, then please purchase your own copy. Refer to the don't-be-a-thieving-asshole section above for clarification. :)

V2

eBook ISBN: 978-1-947093-13-3

Print ISBN: 978-1-947093-14-0

Cover Design by Jayne Rylon

Editing by Mackenzie Walton

Proofreading by Fedora Chen

Formatting by Jayne Rylon

ABOUT THE BOOK

Would it be the worst thing in the world to accept an obscene amount of money in exchange for living with a guy and a couple of his best friends for three months?

Seems like a no brainer. But what if it means sharing their beds, too?

Let's be honest, Holly would probably do that for free considering how hot, successful, and fun to be around they are.

Besides, if she helps Trent cash in on his inheritance—with a few naughty strings attached—she could pay for the life-saving surgery her mother's insurance company has denied.

The one thing she can't afford is falling in love when the man she's obsessed with plans to ditch her after their ninety days are over.

Four Money is book one of the Ever & Always duet. Holly, Trent, Lorenzo, and Owen's story will conclude in Four Love.

ADDITIONAL INFORMATION

Sign up for the Naughty News for contests, release updates, news, appearance information, sneak peek excerpts, reading-themed apparel deals, and more. www.jaynerylon.com/newsletter

Shop for autographed books, reading-themed apparel, goodies, and more www.jaynerylon.com/shop

A complete list of Jayne's books can be found at www.jaynerylon.com/books

1

————

A knock on the door had Holly Hendricks on her feet and lunging toward it before the sound quit ricocheting through her tissue box of a living room. The place was spotless, even more so than usual since she'd been expecting guests for the first time ever.

As Holly bounded past, her mother mustered a wan smile from the thrift store recliner she practically lived in these days. The injustice of it made Holly yank the door open harder than she'd intended. Her messy ponytail brushed her shoulder blades as it swung back and forth in response.

"Holly!" Her best friend from college, Andi, rushed her, threatening to knock them both on their asses with her overenthusiastic embrace.

They twirled around off-balance for a spin or two as they hugged out all the time and miles they'd spent apart. Their lives had diverged so drastically, it would have been easy to lose contact. Yet, somehow, they had grown even closer as a result of their near constant texting, which also included...

"Kari!" Holly shook one arm free of Andi's clutch to include the other woman in their circle. Kari had started out as Andi's friend, but now the three of them were a unit. They'd each been through a lot in the past few years, and having the pair of them as a sounding board was probably the only thing keeping Holly sane given the pressures she was under dealing with her mother's medical crisis.

Andi looked up, her eyes bright. "This place is so..."

"I know." Holly grimaced, trying not to fidget as she imagined how dismal it must be compared to the apartment Andi shared with her three lovers, each of them well on their way to establishing themselves in their chosen professions. She didn't even allow herself to imagine the penthouse Kari occupied with her trio of hotshot lawyer boyfriends. Probably couldn't, to be honest. She'd never been around that kind of true wealth.

"...cute!" Andi finished. Though she was eternally optimistic, only Andi would see the bright side of this dump. It wasn't even as big as the apartment Holly had shared with some friends, above Andi, Cooper, Reed, and Simon's apartment while they'd been in college.

And afterward, when her friends had been climbing the corporate ladder, she'd been sliding down a slippery chute toward poverty and never attaining her goals. Student loan debt for a degree she couldn't use was a monthly reminder of how she'd wasted her time and effort just so she could wind up right where she started, except with more obstacles than before.

That wasn't fair.

Holly glanced at her mom and smiled. She damn well

knew any time they got to spend together was more precious than building a career or accumulating material possessions or meeting a guy…or three, in both Andi's and Kari's cases.

"Holly has done such a great job with it, hasn't she?" Her mother beamed, her quiet pride easy to hear in the intimate space. "The colors make it seem like it's brighter than it really is."

"She has." Andi broke from their circle to approach Holly's mom, Catherine. She must be nearly unrecognizable from the woman who had helped Holly move in and out only a few short years ago. Unlike some people, Andi didn't let Mom's illness put her off. "How are you, Momma C?"

"A pain in the ass, as always." Mom patted Andi's hand. "Don't listen to what Holly tells you. I'm not going anywhere just yet."

"Good to know." Andi smiled, then straightened.

"It's so nice to meet you." Kari was right there to take her place, leaning down to hug Mom. "Technically to meet you both, though from the group chat we're exchanging messages in a million times a day, I feel like I've known Holly forever."

If the other two women noticed the wheeze that accompanied Mom's laugh, they politely ignored it. "I bet. I hear her phone buzzing constantly and she's always tapping on her phone while we're watching TV."

"Sorry, Mom." Holly winced.

"That's not how I meant it." She turned serious then. "I'm glad you have these girls to vent to. I've put too much stress on your shoulders for any one person, especially a daughter."

"It's fine. You know I don't mind." Holly didn't. Really.

But it was a lot to deal with.

The medical bills. The doctor appointments they couldn't afford. The terror that one day she'd wake up and her mom would be too still in the recliner because she couldn't pay for the treatment she needed to fully recover.

"That's because you're the world's best daughter. And that's also why I want you to go have fun with your friends while they're in town." Her mother sat up a little straighter, as if prepared to argue. "Take a mini vacation, Holly. You deserve it. You *need* it."

"What? Mom, you know I can't leave you here alone—"

"You go have fun." Her mother's insistence might have been a little harder to dismiss if she could vigorously fan her hand between them and the door instead of limply mimicking the gesture. "You told me they invited you to the get-together they're holding at one of the fancy hotels on the strip. It sounds great. Don't miss it because of me."

"Parties aren't my thing." Holly shook her head.

"They used to be." Andi might look sweet, but she was more tenacious than a pit bull dismembering a squeaky toy. "And this is going to be a hell of a lot better than getting drunk off cheap liquor at the frat house next door. I mean, not that we ever did that, Momma C."

"What I don't know..." Her mother grinned, but it dimmed quickly. "You haven't had time to cut loose in forever. Go, Holly. Ms. Edison next door said she'd come sit with me if you want some time to yourself. Take tonight off from me and from the misery I've put you through. Hell, take the whole weekend."

"Mom..."

"Don't *mom* me, Holly." Her mother's eyes grew steely, and Holly remembered where she'd gotten her grit and determination from. What she possessed was only a fraction of what her mother had herself. How else could she have outlasted the prognosis of every specialist they'd seen?

"Seriously, Holly," Kari added, "you don't want to miss out. My boyfriends are doing it up right. They rented the entire top floor, hired a team of chefs to cook a private meal, and they invited a bunch of their closest friends. They even told me that if you'd allow it, they'd send a home health aide to take care of Momma C."

"They would really do that?" Why were they going to such extremes? And why would they be so generous with her? Was that just the kind of people they were? Lavish and excessive?

Holly tried not to judge, but when she sometimes had to schedule their payments down to the last penny, she couldn't imagine having the wiggle room to drop that kind of cash on strangers.

"Yes, they would," Andi reassured her. "They're great guys and they can afford it. If they offered, let them. We'd love to spend time with you."

Maybe they were right. Maybe just this once, she deserved a treat.

Hopefully seeing how the other half lived wouldn't make her realize how much she was missing out on. She glanced at the rickety table that doubled as a desk. It was piled with statements from the doctors and medical facilities they owed, including the estimate for her mother's needed surgery.

At the rate she was able to put a couple bucks here or there into savings for the transplant... Well, it was going to take her a hell of a lot longer to save the amount she needed to show before they'd give final approval for the procedure than her mom had left. Disappointment threatened to crush her chest, as it had so many sleepless nights lately.

Yes, she needed a break before she lost it completely. If her friends were willing to give her that priceless gift and her mom was okay with it, she was going to accept it.

When Mom reached out to squeeze Holly's hand, she realized there was nothing worth more in the world. After a little bit of time to refresh and get her head on straight, she'd be able to share more quality time with her mother, while they could.

She looked down and said, "Swear you'll call me if you so much as get a hangnail. I'll be right downtown and can come home at any moment. Okay?"

"Promise. Now let them spoil you like I wish I could." Her mom let go.

Guilt washed over Holly, but she smothered it as best she could. It was only for the weekend, not forever. "I'll go pack a bag, but I don't think I have much that's appropriate for hobnobbing with fancy people."

"Oh, please. That's what shopping is for," Kari laughed, and Andi perked up.

Holly held up her hands, backing away from the pair toward the single bedroom in their home, which she used since her mother had decided she was most comfortable in the living room. "I'll make do with what I've got. I probably have a black dress somewhere that might be passable."

"No, seriously," Kari begged. "Andi helped me make a good impression when I was in a similar situation last year. Let me pay it forward. We'll go to the spa, relax, get makeovers, then buy sparkly Vegas-worthy outfits that will drive our guys wild at the party they're throwing.

Who knows, maybe you'll even hit it off with one of their handsome friends."

That sounded as farfetched as a fairy tale to Holly. But she couldn't deny that for just a couple days, it might be nice to pretend happy endings were possible again.

"Listen to them, honey." Her mother would have shoved her out the door if climbing out of the recliner wasn't such a chore.

What the hell? Holly relented. "I guess there's no use in trying to fight the three of you. You're as stubborn as I am."

"And then some." Andi beamed.

"I'll call Ford and let him know you're keeping the aide." Kari high-fived Andi, as if they'd planned this all along.

"*Keeping*?" Holly narrowed her eyes.

"Oh, yeah. Her name is Beth and she's outside." Kari grinned. "Our limo is waiting by the curb too."

"*Limo*?"

Kari shrugged. "You'll get used to it."

"I doubt that." Holly shook her head, then leaned in to hug her mother. "I love you, Mom."

"I love you, too." Her mom pressed lightly on her shoulders. "Now go. Enjoy every minute."

She intended too. Because both of them knew what her mother left unsaid.

Enjoy it while you can.

While she was young and healthy, and while her friends' generosity made it possible for her to have a reprieve, and while her mom was stable enough to even consider leaving behind temporarily. Come Monday, Holly would be back to reality. Their problems would still be there to worry about then.

2

Slot machines chimed and colored lights flashed, but none of the casino sights or sounds prevented Trent from picking out a familiar voice that came from behind him. "There you are."

He raked the chips from his most recent win toward him on the green felt-covered table, stacking them neatly into piles so he could count them all. It was always good to end on a high note.

"Looks like I'm done," he said to the dealer with a grin before swiveling on the stool to face Reed and the other guys with him.

"Don't tell me you haven't crashed yet." Reed chuckled, looking more mature and put together than Trent remembered from their college days, even though it had only been about two years since they'd graduated. Where Reed wore crisp dark denim and a sport coat, Trent slumped lower in his faded jeans—probably the same pair he'd had back when they were neighbors—and hunched his shoulders in his well-loved hoodie. "You stay out all night, every night?"

"It's my job." He tried not to get defensive. It might look like he was pissing away time or money, but he was dead serious about his goals, and this was one of the fastest ways to reach them.

"Damn. Most days we're in bed before the ten o'clock news," Simon said with his usual good humor. The guys weren't judging Trent. They never did. Hell, they didn't exactly live a traditional life either.

"Can't help it if you got old and boring," Trent teased.

"I didn't say we were sleeping. Spending time with Andi is *never* dull." Cooper nodded at Reed's innuendo. Behind Cooper, another three guys muttered their agreement. If his old college buddies had spiffed up a bit, that trio was next-level entirely. Trent tried not to be intimidated by the presence of the friends of his friends. After all, he'd been like them once. "When are you going to find someone special and settle down?"

"Those kinds of luxuries aren't a part of my plan." Hell, it had been so long since he'd contemplated having an actual girlfriend, the concept seemed foreign to him. He was focused on the future and only allowed himself a periodic hookup as what amounted to a living sex toy used to delight one of the women his roommates Owen and Lorenzo brought home, if the opportunity presented itself. Trent stepped aside so Reed, Simon, Cooper and the three other men they'd brought with them could take stock of his winnings. "Have to do what I can to get ahead, you know?"

Cooper whistled. "Not a bad night's work."

"I always knew you rocked at math, but damn, it looks like those statistics classes are really paying off now," Simon added. "I take back all the shit I talked when you were hitting the books and I wanted to party instead."

"I'd much rather be using my business classes, but...all in due time." He pocketed his chips and stood, clutching Reed in a one-armed hug while Simon and Cooper slapped his back.

When they'd finished greeting each other and talking some mild shit, Reed introduced him to the guys watching them with wide grins. "Trent, I'd like you to meet some of our other friends, who also happen to be Cooper's bosses at the law firm. This is Ford, Brady, and Josh."

They wore jeans too, but with button down shirts, as if they didn't own T-shirts, and their leather shoes were definitely a cut above his own scuffed sneakers. When Ford stuck his hand out to shake, a sleek gold watch winked in the halogen lights.

Oh yeah, they were high rollers all right. Whales big enough to make Trent look like a guppy.

Of course, the fact that they'd flown Trent's friends to Vegas on a private jet for some wild weekend party probably would have been enough proof of that.

Hopefully they truly turned out to be as cool as Reed had assured Trent they were and they wouldn't look down their wealthy noses at him. Not only at him, but especially at his roommates. Trent had spent most of his life around privileged people. Their money didn't faze him, but their personalities might.

"Nice to meet you," Ford said with a smile. And when they shook, he didn't try to outdo Trent in some kind of unreciprocated pissing match like his own asshole father had coached him to do when meeting the bastard's partners, even as a child.

"You too. All of you." With the introductions complete, Trent asked, "Still want some help getting things organized for tonight?"

"If you wouldn't mind." Brady nodded. "We're hoping to make it a special occasion."

"Of course not. My roommates are in too. Owen's shift is just about over, come on." Trent led the guys through the obstacle course the various games made of the casino floor, blanketed by garish carpet that hid too many stains. He wouldn't miss this. As soon as he'd saved enough money, he'd retire his frequent player card for good.

The first breath of quasi-fresh air he sucked in from the parking garage helped him relax. And when he saw Owen joking around with the other valets on duty, he settled even more. He hadn't realized how much the thought of meeting Cooper's rich bosses had set him on edge.

He preferred to ignore any reminders of his past and his judgmental, filthy-fucking-rich family.

Owen was thinner than him and taller too. The guy had a deceptively wiry build that he hid beneath his uniform. He was a fighter, a scrapper, a survivor. A kid who'd grown up exactly opposite of Trent, and yet had ended up in the same place. At least Owen was on his way up while Trent had tumbled.

And as they approached him, so did their third roommate.

Lorenzo strode up to the valet stand, his long dark hair fluttering in the blasts of air that rushed out of the casino every time the giant glass doors slid open. Trent had never seen someone better suited to his job as a male stripper. He owned it, made women scream for him, and loved every dollar bill they slid into his leather G-string.

Trent didn't mind when the guy brought adventurous women home from his club for them to share either. A definite perk of their friendship.

"Owen, Lorenzo…" He lifted his hand and drew them toward him. "These are my friends Cooper, Reed, and Simon. And their friends, Josh, Brady, and Ford. We're going to be helping them out with their shindig tonight."

"Good thing it's my night off." Lorenzo beamed. "It's been a while since I've been to a decent party."

"Well, we're going all out. We want this to be one people talk about for years to come, even by Vegas standards. And we're happy to pay you for your time, of course," Ford offered.

Trent did some crazy shit for money, but he wasn't that greedy. That was what separated him from his father. "Nah, man. We appreciate you bringing these guys out here to hang with. I've missed them and I'm happy to spend time with the old gang. Thanks, though."

Lorenzo scanned them from their shiny shoes to Ford's watch and must have come up with the same findings Trent had. "Are you investors?"

"Nah. Worse, we're lawyers." Josh laughed. The guy seemed less stodgy than Trent would have figured for a partner in a prestigious firm, but it made it damn hard not to like him. Self-made and didn't take himself too seriously. All positives, as far as he was concerned.

"Oh, too bad." Lorenzo wrinkled his nose. "Trent has this awesome idea he should be shopping around."

"For what?" Cooper asked.

"Not worth getting into." Trent glared at Lorenzo. He wasn't trying to shake down his friends' friends. Besides he hadn't yet been able to earn enough to file his provisional patent on his solar battery technology, so he didn't particularly enjoy discussing it in too much detail, especially in public or around people he'd just met.

As always, Owen noticed their rough edges and

smoothed things over. "Yeah, I'm done with working for today. Time to play. So tell me, how many pretty girls are going to be at these festivities tonight?"

The guys laughed, and then Ford answered, "To tell you the truth, I think we've only invited a few. Our girlfriends and a friend of theirs. Maybe a couple clients who live in the area. Think we should expand the guest list?"

"I can sweeten the pot if you want. There is no shortage of gorgeous women looking for fun in Vegas." Lorenzo grinned. "It's the thing I like most about this place."

"I thought you liked getting paid to take your clothes off and shake your ass the best," Owen teased.

"That part doesn't suck either." He laughed twice as hard at the widened eyes of their guests. Then he shrugged. "Hey, at least I'm not a gambler. I work hard for my money."

"I don't want to hear it. From either of you," Owen grumbled.

"Oh, like you don't enjoy driving the exotic cars guests drop off for valet?" Trent knocked his shoulder into Owen.

"Yeah, I think of every parking job as a test drive so I know what I want when you become a bazillionaire and buy me a ride for Christmas one year." He grinned. "Come on, let's get out of here. We have a party to plan."

With that, the nine of them headed toward the ritzy hotel across the street where their whole lives would change, even if they didn't realize it yet.

3

———

Holly had never felt so glamorous or so unrecognizable. They'd been pampered, painted, and fancied up for hours. For fuck's sake, she'd even let Andi and Kari talk her into getting her legs waxed, along with some delicate real estate farther north. It wasn't like anyone was going to know or care besides her, but she admitted she'd always wondered what it would feel like.

Answer: it fucking hurt, but was also kind of...nice. It made her very aware of the silk lingerie she was wearing, and for a moment she wished for someone to show it off to later.

Tonight, it was easy to forget about her problems because she felt like an entirely different woman. She took a quick selfie so at least she could prove to her mom that she was capable of looking like a grown up with a hell of a lot of help. She fired off a text with the image as an attachment asking, *How are you doing?*

Her mother responded immediately. *Everything's fine.*

Enjoy your night and quit worrying about me. Now no more texts. P.S. You look beautiful.

She might, but that didn't keep her from tugging at the black sequined sheath that hugged the equally obsidian lace she wore beneath it. For such a delicate-looking undergarment, it worked some serious magic, molding her shape into something that seemed airbrushed but obviously was not.

On the other hand, Kari appeared perfectly comfortable in the glamorous beaded red gown she'd chosen for herself at the up-scale boutique she'd taken Holly and Andi to, courtesy of her boyfriends' diamond-studded debit card. In fact, it was more than that. Where Holly felt like an imposter, Kari seemed confident and downright radiant.

"You know, this has been a lot. Maybe I should go lie down in your room for a few..." she whispered to Andi.

"You need a couple minutes to rest?" her old friend asked.

"No, hours." Holly winced. "I'm just not sure I'm up for this. I won't fit in. Don't belong. I'm still the same inexperienced yahoo I was when you took pity on me in the campus bookstore freshman year while I tried to figure out the difference between a study guide and a workbook."

Andi hugged her. "You look incredible. This isn't my world either. Or wasn't until recently. But I promise you, Kari's guys are regular people despite their heaps of money."

"Other than the fact that they like to share their woman, right?" Holly reached out and put her hand on Andi's arm. "Sorry. I didn't mean that like it sounded. I know that's how things are with you, Reed, Simon, and

Cooper too. I'm thrilled you're all so happy even if I'm a little jealous. It's just that I feel really, *really* out of my league."

Hell, she hadn't even had a single steady boyfriend since their junior year in college, never mind a handful of them at once.

"I forgive you." Andi put her fingers over Holly's and squeezed. "Trust me. You might feel that way, but you're not. Give it a try at least. I'm sure you're going to have a great time. But if you don't, I'll bail with you. We can hang out, order room service, and stay up all night watching cheesy chick flicks instead as soon as Kari's guys...uh... Well, I have a feeling tonight is going to be special for her. I want to be there. Then after, we can take off if you still want to."

Holly's gaze whipped to her friend's as her eyes narrowed. That sounded oddly specific. Was something going on here that she didn't know about? Maybe this wasn't the casual billionaire jaunt to live it up in Sin City for a weekend as she'd thought. Oddly, it made her feel better to know it might be a special occasion and not an everyday occurrence for them to be this over the top.

In that case, she felt honored to be included in whatever scheme they were devising.

She would have demanded more answers, except just then Kari emerged from the bathroom of the spa where they'd finished getting ready. "Everyone set?"

Before Holly could say no, Andi responded for them both. "Absolutely. I can't wait to see our guys. We look sexy AF. They're going to regret having an all-night rager lined up."

"I guarantee you at least one of my three is going to try to sneak off for a quickie. I don't intend to cave until I can have them together at the end of the night." Kari twirled and laughed. "When did I get to be so damn greedy? Is this really my life?"

Funny, Holly was thinking the same thing, though she was only visiting for an evening. She'd have to remember not to get too used to this since her carriage would officially become a pumpkin again after midnight. And by carriage she meant an Uber, because she didn't own a car.

Kari's, however, would not. The bitch. And she meant that in the nicest possible way.

Kari took her hand then Andi's too, and led them toward the private elevator up to the penthouse. "Who knows, Holly? Maybe we can find you a stud to hook up with. What happens in Vegas…"

"Yeah *stays in Vegas* doesn't really work for me. I live here, remember? The last thing I need is the ghost of a one-night stand haunting me every time I'm out at the grocery store or taking my mom to a doctor's appointment." Holly frowned. "Besides, meeting someone would require mingling with a bunch of strangers and I suck at that."

"Actually, there might be a few people you know here tonight." Andi cleared her throat. The way she looked a bit too casual as she said it, while inspecting the perfect manicure she'd gotten earlier, set Holly on red alert.

"Like who?"

"Reed invited a few friends from college who live in the area." Andi peeked up from beneath thick, dark lashes. She looked even more smoking hot than usual with the sophisticated enhancements their stylists had wrought. That coy glance might work on her boyfriends, but not Holly.

"*Who*, Andi?"

"One guy lived next door to us our senior year. His name is Trent. He was the—"

"Arrogant asshole from the frat house who thought he was hot shit." Holly's eyes nearly rolled so far back she could read the memories of him burned into her brain. "That guy is such a loser."

"I mean, he kind of *was* hot shit. I see you haven't forgotten him," Andi teased.

How could Holly after what she'd stumbled across that one night? Instead of elaborating, she grunted, making a mental note to steer clear of him lest he have yet another chance to completely ignore and disregard her as he had back then. She didn't need that kind of bullshit in her life.

But before the women could debate Trent's merits or shortcomings, the elevator doors opened and they emerged into the heart of the party, Kari in front with Andi, and Holly flanking her. The deep throb of sultry bass pulsated against her sternum, her mouth began to water from the smell of the food being prepared at stations around the wide-open room, and—directly in front of them—the panoramic view of the bustle, fountains, and desert that made Vegas iconic had her blinking back tears.

It was so beautiful from up here. Holly wished she could have shared it with her mother. She'd have to sneak another picture when no one was looking so she didn't blow her faux-sophisticated cover.

As if they could sense Kari's presence, Ford, Brady, and Josh turned from where they'd been chatting with a group of other equally fine men, who stared as Kari sashayed over to them. Meanwhile, Holly did her best not to trip as

Andi took her hand and led her straight to her own boyfriends.

From the corner of her eye, she caught Ford, in a perfectly tailored suit, messing up Kari's artfully applied lipstick as he claimed her mouth before handing her off to his best friends so they could do the same while he watched. It seemed so natural and so damned passionate, along with romantic, that Holly was even more envious of their connection than she'd been of their ability to pay for anything they desired.

After a similar greeting from her lovers, Andi blinked slowly, then shook her head as if trying to remember her manners. The trio of unclaimed men in between Andi and Kari's guys shifted their focus from the very public displays of affection her friends were engaging in to her.

Holly squirmed under their combined attention, but there was nowhere to hide from the warm gaze of the tall man with long, dark hair or the appraising glance of the trim guy with the wry grin beside him. Or...Trent, who happened to be staring at her.

Was it because he was trying to figure out where he knew her from or because he was shocked that she didn't look like the mousey girl who'd orbited the periphery of his life on campus?

Andi covered for her when she couldn't seem to introduce herself. "Trent, you remember my friend, Holly Hendricks?"

Trent's slow, wide smile made Holly positive that even if she hadn't been very memorable, he had gotten off on that one particular unfortunate time their paths had crossed, despite having never mentioned it after that night. Gross.

"Howdy, ex-neighbor." When he stuck his hand out to

shake hers, she ignored it, instead leaning in to hug Simon, one of Andi's boyfriends. He was safe. And definitely not a creeper.

He seemed a little surprised but didn't let her down. "Nice to see you again, Holly. I'm so glad you could make it. I know Andi misses hanging out with you."

He was easygoing and cheerful as ever.

Nothing like intense, and decidedly jerkish Trent.

"It was mostly due to Kari's guys that I could join you." She smiled over at Ford then, still doing her best to act like Trent and the men with him didn't exist. "Thank you, the three of you, for making this possible. The nurse for my mom and all the rest, really, it was beyond generous."

"You're very welcome." Ford beamed at her as he still clasped Kari's hand. If Trent glowered hearing that they'd taken care of her, then she mentally thanked them a second time. "It means a lot that you would take time away from your family, especially given the circumstances, which I'm very sorry to hear about, to share this evening with us."

Holly bit her lip and nodded, coaching herself not to get emotional and screw up her makeup. Unlike Kari, she wouldn't know how to fix it.

Glancing between Andi, Kari, and the men standing tall behind each of them, it was tough not to feel like some people had all the luck. If she had any, it was the bad kind.

Before she could let that bitterness fester, she shook it off and smiled at her friends. "Well, you two kept talking about how much you wanted to dance tonight. Don't let me stifle your fun. I'll still be here after you get reunited with your guys."

"I see why you like her. She's smart." Brady tugged Kari toward the gleaming parquet floor where people were already swaying to the music in the diffused lighting, which allowed the glory of the Vegas sunset behind them to glow throughout the room, lending a gold cast to everything it touched.

"I'll be back," Kari called over her shoulder.

"Mind if we borrow Andi for a few minutes too?" Cooper asked Holly.

Andi tried to object, to explain that she didn't want to abandon her guest, but while Holly appreciated her friend's efforts, she wasn't about to be the third—or fifth—wheel either. "Go ahead. I'll scout out the food and let you know what's good once you've worked up an appetite."

Andi winked at her. "We're only going to be dancing. For now."

Trent and the other two guys left behind cracked up at that as her friends wandered off.

While they were distracted, Holly slipped away, making good on her promise. She'd been too excited to eat much of the gourmet appetizers offered at the spa. If she didn't have something soon she was likely to pass out when she kicked off the only pair of designer heels she would ever likely own and joined her friends on the dance floor later.

As she neared the expansive window, she paused to take in the final moments of the sunset, snapping a photo and texting it to her mother with the caption *just one more...* Tipping her face into the sunlight, she savored its warmth and beauty. She might have been alone in the sea of strangers, but how could she not appreciate splendor as intense as that?

Living there day in, day out, stuck in her tiny apartment with hardly any windows—and certainly none with a view like this—she had forgotten to look around for a while.

Andi and Kari had been right. There was more to life than the desperation and impotency she wallowed in daily. Tonight she was going to live it up and experience every bit of joy she could to hold her over when she returned to her duties, taking care of her mom.

Hell, maybe she'd change her mind and hook up with one of the rich dudes circling the room like extraordinarily well-dressed sharks. More than one cast her not-so-subtle glances that she caught in the reflection on the window.

When the sun disappeared behind the red mountains and the lights of the strip dancing like fallen stars took center stage, Holly pressed her hand to her rumbling stomach, then turned toward the nearest food station.

It wasn't until she had already made eye contact—so she couldn't politely bail—that she realized the placard describing the offerings that could be prepared personally for you by the probably-famous chef was written entirely in French.

Shit.

She should have known she would be too far out of her league to manage solo. She nibbled her lower lip, about to pick something at random—because, really, how bad could it be compared to the ramen noodles she usually existed on?—when someone came up behind her. Perfect. She could step aside and let them go first, under the guise of making up her mind. And if whatever they chose didn't still have eyeballs or look like fried brains, she'd ask for the same.

Except when she turned to invite the other guest to go first, she realized it was Trent.

Damn it. Well, even engaging in small talk with him was better than making a complete fool of herself.

And if she was being honest, he didn't make her drool any less than the aroma of the five-star cuisine awaiting them. He was tall, and his face had lost some of its youthful fullness, chiseling a sinfully handsome man from the attractive guy he'd been. His neon-blue eyes cut to hers and seemed to stare deeper than she was comfortable with.

"I didn't get to say hello earlier," he said, more gently than she would have thought possible from his crass and usually drunk days at university. Besides, he actually had even if she'd pretended not to hear. "You look amazing."

"Thank you." She tried not to be too clipped, but she hated the part of herself that reacted to his compliment like a dog whose ears perked up when someone rattled a treat bag. So what if she'd always wished he'd notice her before he'd shown her his true, dirty colors?

Those days were long gone.

"You want to go ahead? I'm not sure what I want yet." She waved toward the menu.

Part of her chuckled, wondering how he was going to handle the situation. But her jaw dropped when he perused the list for a few moments then said, in what sounded like pretty perfect French to her, *"Bonsoir. Je voudrais le foie gras de canard et l'antilope enveloppée de bacon, s'il vous plaît."*

"What the hell did you just say?" she hissed before she could think better of it.

When he caught her shocked expression, he glowered. "I'm not just a dumb frat boy."

"Well, if you think not knowing French makes you stupid, then I guess I am." She turned to go, suddenly not hungry anymore. Now she was ignorant as well as unworthy of younger-him's notice.

Fuck that.

His hand flashed out and cupped her upper arm, preventing her from leaving. "Hey. Sorry. That's not what I meant. Can I help you pick something you'll enjoy for dinner?"

Holly wished she could stick her nose up at his offer, but damn it, her stomach was practically digesting itself by now and whatever the chef was preparing looked and smelled amazing.

So she swallowed her pride and nodded.

Trent shifted his gaze to the menu again and began to read each line to her without a moment of hesitation. There wasn't anything on it he didn't know, either. Even better, he did it discreetly, as if they were discussing the options, so that everyone else around didn't figure out what he already knew about her lack of sophistication. And damn if that—along with his tight ass in his clean and well-pressed jeans—didn't make her find him that much more attractive.

When he got to seared scallops in a white wine sauce, she nearly moaned. "That. I'd like that, please."

He grinned, then placed her order with the chef before turning to lean his hip against the counter. "So this is some pretty fancy shit, huh? Can you imagine, our neighbors have really come up in life, huh? How about you? What are you doing these days?"

Living at home, watching my mom die.

Okay, so even she wasn't that socially inept.

"Nothing as impressive as any of this. I've had some setbacks. Life happened, you know?" She sighed.

"I do." Even the slight crinkles that developed around

his mouth when his smile turned into a much more solemn expression were sexy, damn him.

She'd never seen him be so somber in the entire four years they'd lived in the same neighborhood. And she didn't like being the cause of his changed attitude right then. "Anyway, Andi said you work out here too. What do *you* do?"

"I play cards." He shrugged.

"I meant for a living." She couldn't imagine having enough extra money to risk it on gambling.

"So did I."

Ah, shit. So much for that. Holly could never find someone so irresponsible and cavalier about finances attractive. To be clear, she thought he was insanely fuckable. Hell, he'd shown her just how good he was in bed, or a flower bush, during that party that had spilled outside into the yard between their houses. Just not anything more than that.

Kari had found not one but three guys to bring financial stability and passion into her life. Andi was paving her own way along with her trio of hotties. They might not be wealthy like Kari's three, but they had worked hard to be secure on top of having the intangible stuff that mattered, you know, like true love.

With a guy like Trent, all she'd have was a quick, highly satisfying romp in some shady corner.

Though that could be what she needed this weekend.

The chef handed their plates over and Trent took them both, carrying them toward one of the black linen-topped tables. She should have grabbed hers and run, but her aforementioned stilettos weren't exactly intended for evasive maneuvers and no way in hell was she risking that incredible meal tumbling to the carpet along with her bruised ego.

"Eat with me?" He pulled out a chair for her as if he were a gentleman instead of the scoundrel she knew him to be. It was a far cry from a campus cafeteria, and yet she realized it didn't mean anything more to him than a chance run-in with a classmate would have.

"No, thanks." She looked around for the guys he'd been with when she'd arrived, but they seemed to be off dancing. If they minded that women were in the minority at this soiree, it certainly didn't show. They had trapped a single lady between them as they bumped and grinded. The man with long hair especially had a flair for moving to the music.

"Yeah, my roommates aren't coming back any time soon." Trent huffed. "Come on, let me stay. I won't bite. I mean, I realize I didn't make the best first impression on you back in our college days…"

Oh, it had been *quite* the impression all right. The number of times she'd fantasized about being the woman he'd fucked up against the exterior wall of the frat house, poorly concealed by some rhododendrons that had recently been trimmed, would probably surpass the tally of people sipping free drinks in Vegas right then.

He had looked up, seen her, and smiled while never missing a beat. From the wild moans of the woman he'd been riding, he'd been doing a good job of it too. So why hadn't he even cared that she had spied them? And why hadn't he ever mentioned it in the months afterward when their paths had seemed to crisscross constantly?

Frankly, she'd assumed he'd been too drunk at the time to remember later, but clearly that wasn't the case at all. That alone made him the sort of man she shouldn't care to spend one moment longer with than necessary.

"Stay, please. It's always bugged me that I didn't apologize for being such a dirtbag and for getting off on you seeing...well, what you saw." He cleared his throat.

"You *liked* me watching you?" Her fork clattered to her plate before she scooped it up and sank onto the chair he'd held out for her.

Again pretending that he had manners, he scooted her chair in and handed her a cloth napkin before taking the seat next to her.

"You couldn't tell?" He scrubbed his hand over his face, then asked, "Do you want a drink? I think I'm going to need one if we keep talking about this."

Holly didn't usually knock them back, but she figured the evening—and the discussion they were about to have —might call for one, or three. "Do you think they have beer? Or is that too tame for this crowd?"

Trent's smile lit up his whole face and turned his eyes from overcast to a clear summer day. "At a soiree like this, I'm pretty sure they'd brew it for you if they didn't already have a dozen on tap to choose from. I'll be right back. And I'll grab some dessert too."

As he strode toward the open bar by way of a tower of chocolate heaven, she wondered how Trent suddenly came off as the world's most perfect man. Tight ass in those jeans included. Maybe they should change the saying to *What happened on the strip...*"\

Because she had a feeling she was about to take a walk even further on the wild side than she already had that evening. And suddenly she was looking forward to the journey.

4

Trent scrubbed his hand through his hair. Holly fucking Hendricks. Of all the women he hadn't expected to see that night, it had to be her. The sweet girl he had known better than to touch, no matter how desperately he'd wanted to, when he was too busy fooling around to be committed to anyone.

And now?

What about now?

He had even less to offer someone than he had a few years ago, before he'd discovered the darker part of himself and had been banished from his father's house, life, and trust fund for embracing it.

Hell, look at how scandalized Holly had been peeping on him fucking that beautiful girl who'd been his lab partner and whose name he should definitely be able to think of, but couldn't. How fast would she run if she knew the truth about his desires?

Then again...she was here with Andi and Kari, wasn't she?

She had to have some idea what they were into.

Maybe the classy woman she'd grown into didn't bat an eye when it came to liaisons that included more than one lover. Somehow he didn't quite believe that, no matter how desperately he wished it was true and that someone like her could accept someone like him for more than a single night of pleasure.

Trent held the necks of two beers easily in one hand so he could snag a slice of chocolate raspberry cake with the other, then headed back to where she waited, her eyes closed as she savored a taste of the lush dinner they'd scored.

While he'd forsaken most of the things he'd grown up with, he had to admit, he'd missed a few extravagances, like the grub here tonight. And he planned to enjoy it, with Holly. As long as he could convince her that he wasn't the scum she'd always assumed.

Fuck him, he was going to have to try to remember how to be charming. Or at least reveal a tiny bit of how much he desired her. It had been a while since he'd allowed himself to be vulnerable, but with Holly, that was probably his only shot.

And suddenly, he didn't want to go home alone that night.

Or with a woman one of his friends scored for him.

But would Lorenzo and Owen be into her even if she wasn't one of the party girls they were used to? And would she let them rock her world like he knew they could?

That was a whole lot of getting ahead of himself.

Trent returned to the table, flashing her a lopsided smile as he set their drinks and dessert down. "Look, Holly. Can I cut to the chase? I meant what I said before. Yeah, I got off on you watching that night, mostly because I wished it was you in those bushes with me."

"Me?" Instead of being outraged or shocked, she laughed. If she wasn't so gorgeous that it nearly stunned him stupid, he might have cringed.

His brows knit as he realized she honestly thought he was joking. "Quit it. I'm serious."

He took such a long draw from his beer that he downed nearly half the thing in one pull. He wasn't sure he could handle another epic failure. This was his shot to make at least one of his past mistakes right, even if it was only for a single, incredible evening.

Holly looked like she might choke on her next bite of scallop. Her eyes widened as she studied the artfully arranged plate, avoiding his gaze. So he dropped his hand to her knee and squeezed. "I'm sorry I didn't tell you then how attractive you always were to me, not only for your looks, but because of the way you dedicated yourself to studying and how passionately you talked about your goals with Andi on the back deck while you two were sunbathing on Sunday afternoons..."

She frowned at that and stabbed something on her plate. Because he'd paid too much attention to her sexy body laid out to catch the sun's rays or because she might not have achieved all she'd dreamed of just yet?

Shit, he had never been very good at this heart-to-heart bullshit. That's why he'd stuck to seduction, which he excelled at. He smiled as he remembered another gift she'd given him, even if she didn't know it. "And how fierce and protective you were the night just before graduation when you came to our place with that lost puppy you'd found, refusing to quit until you'd knocked on every door in the neighborhood, looking for its home."

Holly did look up at him from beneath thick lashes and golden eyes he'd never properly appreciated until that instant. Maybe because of the shimmery makeup highlighting them, but probably because he hadn't taken the opportunity to really look before. He'd been so stupid.

"You wouldn't let me go by myself."

He nodded. "It was late and there were young, stupid, drunk frat guys around."

She raised an artfully arched brow.

"Yeah, like me." He shrugged. He deserved it.

"I remember how tiny he looked in your hands when you agreed to keep him until morning when the shelter opened, since my landlord didn't allow pets." Holly licked her lips and leaned forward, her eyes widening as she met his gaze.

Yes! It wasn't his imagination. She felt the pull between them too. "He was a cute one."

"Yes, he was." She smiled, her shoulders loosening as she finally relaxed around him, maybe for the first time ever. So he didn't screw it up by talking. Instead, they ate in peace, enjoying the music, the meal, and the comfort of having someone familiar, yet interesting, nearby.

And when they'd finished, he asked, "Would you like to try something else? Or maybe dig in to this cake with me?"

She surprised him by finishing off her beer then shooting to her feet, as if afraid she might not do it if she didn't right that instant. "Yes, I would like to try something else."

"Okay, what?" He stood too, glancing at the remaining stations, dropping his folded napkin on the table before bracing her with one hand on the dip of her waist when she wobbled in her mile-high heels, which highlighted her incredibly long, sexy legs.

"You."

His cock liked the sound of that, stirring in his jeans. It took everything he had to contain his wolfish grin, and he wasn't sure he'd entirely succeeded.

She flushed and put her hand on her cheek. "I mean. Dancing. With you."

Trent was no Lorenzo, but he'd lived with the guy—seen him practicing in their living room and partied with him—long enough to pick up a few pointers here and there. He could hold his own. And anything that would put him in closer contact with Holly got an enthusiastic thumbs-up.

"Come on, I love this song." She laced his fingers with her own, then led him to the dance floor.

The warmth of her smaller hand tucked in his, lit him on fire. "So do I."

It had become an instant favorite now that he knew he was about to share it with her.

It didn't surprise him that as soon as she decided to give in to whatever magic was brewing between them, the illicit vibe of a party being thrown by three polyamorous men in honor of the woman who'd ensnared their hearts —and, let's be honest, their dicks too—and the latent desire that had always existed between them, Holly became a complete siren.

Lights glinted off the black sequins of her dress, making her look like some kind of exotic cobra mesmerizing its handler as she swayed to the heavy beat. Trent gathered her to him as he matched the pace she set, completely in tune with her rhythm.

His stomach sank when she pulled away, until he realized it was only so she could spin in his arms, pressing her ass to his groin as she shimmied against him. It had to be obvious what she was doing to him. His cock hardened against her.

With his arm around her middle, hugging her tight to him, not only was it impossible to miss the effect she had on him, but she also had a direct line of sight to Lorenzo and Owen, who were edging closer to where they were bumping and grinding on the dance floor.

Trent dipped his head and nuzzled her neck beneath the waterfall of gentle curls her hair had been styled into. Then he said, loud enough for her to hear over the music, "Mind if they join us?"

He didn't have to wait long for his answer. Holly peeked up at him with a grin before raising her hand and curling her fingers toward her palms while leveling his roommates with a brazen stare neither of them would be able to resist.

Sure enough, Lorenzo elbowed Owen. When the other man caught sight of Holly beckoning them, he missed a beat. Just one, though, before dancing in their direction.

Lorenzo did the same, putting on a hell of a show. When he neared he spun around then dropped to his knees, rippling his fucking perfect abs so there was no question of how he'd handle himself in bed. He put his hands on Holly's thighs and looked up at her, making it clear that if her dress wasn't in the way, he'd find something much better to do down there.

Lorenzo got to his feet, still moving to the beat as he made room for Owen to join them, grinning at their friend's over-the-top approach.

With their bodies so close, Trent felt Holly go liquid in his hold, melting into him even more completely than she had before. His hands skimmed up her sides, and he would bet all his winnings from the past week that if he'd been able to see her nipples right then, they'd have been as hard as the diamonds dripping from her friend Kari's ears.

Although he was focused on Holly, and his encroaching roommates, he couldn't help but be blinded by the periodic sparkle from their neighbors on the dance floor.

For the first time in a while, Trent regretted that he didn't have all the resources he used to at his disposal. He had a sudden urge to spoil Holly rotten.

He was going to have to come up with some other plan besides gambling his way to filing his patents and funding his startup. But that was a problem for another time. Nothing was going to distract him from enjoying Holly and how she amplified her movements with each step closer Lorenzo and Owen took.

The four of them ended up dancing together, the three men marking the corners of a triangle where Holly was anchored against him. Lorenzo and Owen each took one side of her front, playing nice together and letting each have a chance to flirt with her and show off.

Trent thought they'd be lucky if he made it off the dance floor without embarrassing himself. The soft swell of her ass was doing wicked things to his hard-on as she swiveled her hips and showed him just how much fun they could have together.

Her and him. Or her, him, and his friends.

This was going to be one of the best nights of his life, he could already tell.

Holly laughed when Lorenzo shimmied in front of her, yet somehow managed to look confident and full of flair instead of cheesy as Trent would have if he'd attempted the same thing. Owen even cracked a smile, forgoing the intense mask he'd been wearing as he took in the sensual aura glowing around their little group.

They were such a good match. A perfect fit.

The three of them together, and now Holly too. It couldn't be this easy, could it?

Trent could have danced with them forever. Except another song didn't follow that one. When the final note died out, he glanced toward the DJ only to see Ford, Brady, and Josh making their way over to him, beaming at the crowd. It was easy to tell Ford was used to speaking publicly when he took the microphone and addressed everyone gathered around. "Thank you for coming tonight. We're so glad to share this special time with you. But, of course, especially with our girlfriend Kari."

Simon whistled while many other people cheered around the room. Cooper clapped and Andi clasped her hands in front of her.

Even Trent felt his throat tighten and his palms begin to sweat. The stakes were impossibly high for his new friends right then. What would it feel like to put all his chips on the line like this?

Especially so publicly.

Trent had been rejected by his own parents. What could make a woman decide to spend her entire life with him? He certainly didn't have as much to offer as Ford, Brady, and Josh. Then again, few men did.

Brady took up where Ford had left off, seeming to need a moment to get his shit together. "We're hoping that we never have to call her that again after tonight. Because she's so much more than that to us."

Kari was caught in a spotlight, everyone's eyes on her, and her jaw was hanging slack.

Despite the crowd looking at her, she was only paying

attention to her guys, and what they were about to say next. The reason they'd brought her to Vegas and assembled their friends to share the moment with them.

Josh stepped forward and took her hand in his, gently, as if she was the most precious thing in their world. And given everything they had, that was saying a lot. Then he knelt. "We love you, Kari. And this time we want to give you a hell of a lot more than a pen to prove it. We want to share everything we have, all of us, with you."

"And this ring," Brady added as he joined Josh.

Ford did too before he asked, "Will you marry us, Kari? Let us be yours forever."

Her free hand flew to her mouth and a single tear splashed down her cheek as if it was a scene from a classic movie with a very modern twist. Then she nodded and flung herself at the men.

They ended up in a not-so-sophisticated heap on the glossy dance floor, not giving a shit that they weren't as poised or perfect as they at first seemed. None of that mattered when they had each other. And in that moment, Trent realized *that* was what he wanted. More than money, his business, or even his parents' approval.

That.

He looked over Holly's head at Lorenzo and then Owen, who nodded before returning their hungry stares to the newly engaged foursome, who were picking themselves up and crushing Kari in a group embrace. Nothing and no one else could intrude on their circle of love, hope, friendship, and solidarity.

At least not until a giant bang startled everyone.

Shimmers of red and gold made the entire room sparkle.

Holly gasped and whipped her stare between her

celebrating friends and the fireworks that began to streak through the night sky. There were so many of them it almost seemed to be raining fire onto the fountains below.

The people in the room lined up so they had front row seats to the most spectacular display he'd ever witnessed. Fireworks silhouetted Kari kissing each of her men before she stood, holding hands with them, as they looked out on the start of their brilliant future together.

Trent didn't even realize he was hugging Holly until she sighed and leaned back against him, her head resting on his shoulder as if she'd been made just for him. Lorenzo and Owen stood on either side of him, cheering at the blasts of light and sound.

And yet, Trent couldn't help himself. Instead of staring at the show, he glanced down at Holly's profile, illuminated by the bursts of warm light. She was the most beautiful woman he'd ever seen, never mind touched, and he didn't plan to let her leave tonight without telling her so.

Hopefully right before she accepted his invitation to make their party a little more—but not *too*—private, at the house he shared with Lorenzo and Owen.

5

Overwhelmed with emotion after witnessing Kari's engagement and the celebratory fireworks, Holly tipped her head up toward Trent, who was cradling her against his hard, hot body.

The fact that she wasn't alone as Kari and Andi celebrated with their guys went a long way toward helping her cheer on her best friends like she always wanted to do but sometimes had trouble managing without a hint of envy.

As if Trent could sense her stare, he glanced down and smiled. But he didn't stop there. The dazzling lights made his eyes glow like neon as he lowered his head and brushed his lips across hers.

Fuck the fireworks outside. Plenty of them were going off in her mind and body as they kissed for the first time. It was every bit as magical as she'd pictured during those nights in her bed as she stared out her window, which faced his. Too bad the gap between their houses and their very different lives had seemed insurmountable then, or maybe she could have done this years ago.

Holly spun around to face Trent so she could get a better taste of him.

He sealed their lips more completely as he groaned and began to devour her. As he did, he walked her backward around a corner into a shadowy nook near the service elevator, away from the crowd and the hundreds of eyes that were admittedly not paying them any attention with such a spectacular distraction in progress.

He tucked her beside some giant palm in a pot and used his body to shield her further. Of course, the only thing she could think of was that she was finally getting her turn—sort of—with him in the bushes.

Trent might have read her mind. He lifted his head long enough to wink at her and laugh before diving in for another kiss. This one a hell of a lot hotter than the innocent exploration they'd shared by the windows.

His hands dropped to her ass, cupping it and using the firm grip to pin her to his pelvis.

The hard length of his cock was even more obvious as it nudged her mound than it had been when he'd been rubbing up against her ass on the dance floor.

Holly reached up, her fingers spearing into his hair. Electricity arced through her, brighter than the fireworks they'd left behind, inspiring her to clench her fists and draw him down so she could deepen their kiss. She couldn't say what got into her, but next thing she knew, she was nipping his lower lip, desperate for him to take things further. To be the guy she had always assumed he was. The kind who would fuck a woman in plain sight if that's what he needed. Because right then, she wouldn't give a damn if he decided to lift the skirt of her dress and satisfy them both, everyone else within a couple hundred feet be damned.

What would she do if one of his roommates came looking for them, or even found them and gawked like she had? Hell, what if they wanted to make out with her too?

Holly moaned. She raised her knee to hook around his hip, not giving a shit when her dress rode up. And with some goading from his hands on her ass, she hopped, wrapping her legs around him.

He leaned in, pinning her against the wall, his lower body smooshed against hers as his mouth and tongue drove her wild. She'd never been kissed like that before, so thoroughly or possessively, and she couldn't say she minded one bit.

For once in her life, Holly realized she could let go. She gave in and trusted Trent to make them both feel good, because no matter what else happened he was extremely capable of that.

Her thoughts evaporated and all she did was experience the moment. The pounding of her heart drowned out her worries. The sweet rush of arousal snuffed out the objections of her better sense. And the sweep of his lips over hers lulled her into relinquishing control.

Until she realized she was lightheaded from more than just the exhilaration of making out with her college crush. She needed to breathe.

Holly tipped her head back, not caring when it clunked against the wall. She gasped as she drew in gulp after gulp of air, with the goal of returning to exactly what they'd been doing as quickly as possible.

"Damn, Holly." He sipped from her lips again as if she was as delicious as the chocolate raspberry torte he'd selected for their dessert. "You have no idea how many times I thought about doing this...and more...with you."

"Then why didn't you?" she wondered.

"I didn't think a girl like you would be into it. Especially not after how you looked down at me after... that night." He cleared his throat. "I'd already gotten into a big fight with my family a few months before that, because they didn't like...well, whatever. I didn't think you'd be into it, or me. It doesn't matter why."

"I think it does." She kissed him again, once, sweetly but drew away before they could get carried away.

"Let's just say they didn't approve of my shenanigans any more than you did. And I think that stung some. Because I assumed you'd be like them. Sorry, though, I should have talked to you about what you saw. That guy... he's not me. Not usually. I was working through some shit, and drinking more than I should have pretty much every weekend. I don't do that anymore. Just so you know."

To be fair, he'd limited himself to the single beer they'd shared over their dinner tonight. Maybe he *was* different. Or possibly he'd never been the person she'd assumed.

Then again, here they were sharing the dimly lit nook as they practically sucked each other's faces off.

Holly had judged Trent pretty harshly, but she was willing to admit, at least to herself, that part of her disdain had been a way to mask her disappointment that he'd never tried to do the same with her. Who could have guessed he'd felt like *he* wasn't good enough for *her*?

Suddenly she wanted to be honest about her emotions, to keep from wasting any more chances. So she cupped his face in her palms and aimed it toward her so he could see the sincerity in her gaze. Except this time, she didn't try to consume him like she had their meal. She savored both his lush lips and his startled expression. Holly kissed him like she meant it, as if they were both the people they had wanted to be before life had gotten in the way.

He groaned and deepened the exchange, though not in some desperate, uncouth fashion. He was suave and seductive and made tingles spread from her toes upward.

When they reached her knees and kept climbing, she got a little unsteady.

He was there, keeping her close to his strong frame so she wouldn't slip down the wall and melt into a puddle of goo at his feet.

"You know, my place isn't that far from here." Trent winced. "It's nothing fancy like this. We could get a room here instead if you want to keep the fairy tale going for the rest of the night..."

"Are you saying you want to spend it with me?" Holly asked, blinking. Now was not the time to presume anything and embarrass the hell out of herself.

"Yeah, I do." He grinned at her. "Before you decide, you should know that Lorenzo and Owen live with me."

"Is that a problem?" She nibbled her lower lip, hoping he couldn't tell that the thought of his friends hearing them fuck definitely didn't turn her off as much as decorum would suggest it should.

"Not for us." He rubbed his cheek against hers and whispered in her ear, "Is it for you?"

But before she was forced to give a candid answer, and admit that she was curious about how that might turn out...someone called their names.

Holly scrambled, unhooking her legs and trying to put her feet back on the ground without her dress bunching up completely at her waist. Her insides fluttered, and not necessarily because they'd been caught.

More because she sort of liked the idea of someone finding them. Of someone knowing that he craved her as intensely as she did him. What the hell was wrong with her?

"Hey, man, there you are." Lorenzo, with his long dark hair and the sexiest walk Holly had ever seen, crashed their party for two. "Shit. Sorry. But I need to talk to you."

"I'm busy. And if you don't fuck this up, you might be later too…" Ignoring the presence of his friend, Trent dipped his head and laid his lips over hers once more. If he cared that the other man was about to get an eyeful, he didn't bother to stop. Was it some kind of test? Did he really mean that she might have the pleasure of hooking up with Trent *and* his hot friends that night?

If so, Holly intended to pass with flying colors, as she had each exam in their college years. She should have realized he didn't mind being watched, hell, he'd admitted he'd gotten off on it. Had he really come harder that night knowing she'd spied him and his date getting busy in the bushes like he implied earlier?

Holly wanted to be that woman, even if only for one moment. One night.

"Let's get out of here," Holly whispered in between his kisses.

"Yeah? Seriously?" He paused long enough to smile wide and slow.

She nodded.

"Trent. I'm serious." Lorenzo put his hand on Trent's shoulder, his fingers damn near brushing her as well. Holly shivered.

"What?" Trent barked, his voice scratchier than she remembered. "Somebody better be dying."

Lorenzo winced and their other roommate—Owen—joined them, his handsome face blanching as he caught the tail end of Trent and Lorenzo's discussion.

"They might be. I mean, *he* might be." Lorenzo scrunched his eyes closed before opening them again. His warm brown gaze met Trent's. "One of the guys from my show saw it on the news. It's your dad. He had a massive stroke and they're not sure if he's going to make it. They're transporting him to Sunrise."

Holly gasped. She clutched Trent so tight she felt every one of his muscles go from loose and languid to knotted in an instant. He'd just gotten the news she dreaded every day of her life.

If there was anything she could do to help him, she would.

Almost one-night stand or not, no one deserved to face something so devastating without as much of a support system as they could muster. And for some reason, maybe it was how he'd cradled that puppy so long ago, she suddenly wanted to take care of him and protect him the same way.

He looked at her, then Lorenzo, then the ceiling. "Fuck!"

Owen put his hand on Trent's other shoulder and squeezed.

"I'll come with you, if you want..." Holly offered.

"You will?" Trent blinked as if he'd never expected in a million years that she or anyone else would go out of their way for him. He really had chosen the wrong women to fool around with, hadn't he?

"Yeah, there might be young, wanton women out here

you need me to protect you from." She echoed his earlier reason for accompanying her that night they'd searched for the puppy's owner or at least his momma dog.

Fortunately, he got her sense of humor even in the freefall moment. The corner of his mouth kicked up. He glided his hands down her sides, subtly rearranging her dress, then linked their hands. "Thank you. I promise I'll make it up to you later."

"I'm sure you will." She wondered how fast she could run in her heels.

"What's happening?" Ford asked as he came around the corner with Kari and his two best friends in tow. They'd apparently had a similar idea about the usefulness of the shady nook.

"Family emergency." Lorenzo winced. "Trent's. Not mine."

Owen slapped the button on the service elevator. "Let's go to the valet stand. I'll make sure they give you the next taxi."

"Take our limo," Ford offered.

"At this time of night it could take a while, even for VIP service." Owen shook his head.

"You two go." Brady winced when Owen slapped the button on the service elevator. "We'll find Reed, Andi, Simon, and Cooper, wait for the limo, and bring them to the hospital so you have some support."

"That's not necessary." Trent lifted his hands, palms out, but Holly could see them trembling. He was going to need as many friends as he could find before the night was through.

"Of course it is." She hugged him tight.

More people started to gather around them as they caught wind of their urgency and worried expressions.

Trent seemed to get more uncomfortable with every ounce of attention and the sympathetic whispers swirling around them.

"Don't ruin everyone's good time. Certainly not because of that bastard..." His passion faded and his fear evaporated as something darker took up residence in his eyes.

Andi cut through the throng milling around with Cooper, Reed, and Simon right behind.

"Is it true?" Cooper asked.

Trent nodded once right before the elevator dinged and the doors slid open. "Holly and I are about to catch a cab to the hospital. Sorry to ruin the party. Congratulations. We've got to go."

Fortunately, he didn't try to stop Holly from leaving with him.

They stepped onto the elevator together.

Owen looked to Ford. "Still want me to get your car?"

"Yes, thanks." He nodded.

"Can we come too in case we can help?" Andi asked, confirming Ford's instincts.

"Please don't." Trent winced. "Enjoy yourselves."

Holly saw the group exchange glances as Owen stepped into the elevator too and kept holding the door. A buzzer sounded since they'd taken too long already.

Brady said what they all were thinking: "Love is about a lot more than the good times. We'll have plenty of those in our lives. It's more important to stick together when things are rough."

"We'll be right behind you," Andi promised. "Go."

Lorenzo joined them right before Owen took his hand off the doors and they clanged closed.

Though it was a long way down from the heights

they'd been at so recently, they dropped fast and stopped with a jolt. Then they were running, Trent clasping her hand so tightly that she knew even if she stumbled, he wouldn't let her fall.

Hopefully she could do the same for him.

6

———

Holly clutched Trent's fingers as the cab rushed them toward the hospital. Although his roommates knew Trent far better than she did, he hadn't let go of her hand for one moment, so she'd held on to him too, hoping the others would be close behind,

There they were, her praying for his father as he sat stock still and ramrod stiff beside her.

Was he in shock?

Why was he so damn quiet?

What should she say?

Holly didn't have long to worry about it because they made it to the hospital in record time. Trent pressed way more cash than it would take to cover their fare into her hand and hopped out before the car had stopped moving. She paid the driver, then raced after Trent through the automatic doors of the emergency room.

When she caught up to him, he was bent over the counter. "I don't care what he said or how he feels about me, he's my father. If he's going to die, I should be able to see him before it's too damn late."

"I'm sorry, sir." The nurse behind the counter flinched, as if expecting Trent to take a swing at her.

Holly might not have been half as composed as him if someone had tried to keep her from being by her mother's side when the time came. A full-body shiver ran down her spine.

The nurse winced as she took in Trent's stony visage and Holly biting her lip as she came up behind him. "I feel for you. I do. I'm just doing my job." The woman frowned. "Let me try again."

She turned her back and whisper-shouted into the receiver of a wired phone with a zillion blinking lights. Then her head hung before she wrapped up the call and turned around. "I'm sorry, sir. He's already gone."

Gone? Holly thought that was the oddest way to put it. Had the man just gotten up and slipped out the door? No. They were telling Trent that his father was dead.

They hadn't made it in time.

He would never get to say whatever it was that he would have murmured or to share those final moments with his parent to ease their transition to...wherever it was he'd *gone.*

"Trent, I'm so sorry." Holly hugged him tight from behind, rubbing his solid abs and chest as he vibrated in her arms. He peeled her off and pivoted in a circle slowly, as if he were lost, before stepping aside into a quiet corner where spare wheelchairs were stashed.

Holly followed, completely unsure of what else to say. Nothing she could think of seemed profound enough. And he wasn't responding to her sympathy anyway. He had more in common with a robot than a grieving man. Was he in shock?

"We all gotta go sometime." His tone was flat,

nothing like the animated way he'd talked to her about their dinner, their time at college, or even that puppy he'd frozen his ass off on a cold spring night to help her save.

Yet, he wasn't breaking down. And when she glanced up at him, she wasn't sure his emotion had anything in common with sorrow. It looked more like anger, his face red and his teeth gnashed.

"Are you...okay?" It was a stupid question. Of course, he couldn't possibly be all right. But what exactly was he? She didn't know him well enough to guess.

"Yeah." He looked up at the ceiling and blew out a breath.

"You sure?" She had no idea how to handle him or what was coming next, but she expected him to crumble at any moment.

He didn't.

So she just kept staring at him, unblinking, waiting for something that never happened.

"I'm fine," he promised, though it couldn't be the truth.

"Trent..." Holly reached out again, but he jerked back, shaking his head at her.

"What am I supposed to do, fucking cry?" Trent shouted, his hands flung out. "Because he died or because he hated his own son so much he didn't even want to say goodbye?"

Holly stumbled back a step and then another. There was no world in which she could imagine it being her mother in there on that cold, steel table and her own eyes being dry. Hell, she'd bawled herself to sleep dozens of nights over the fear of it alone.

"That bastard! Good riddance." Trent kicked one of

the wheelchairs, toppling it and several others. "Fuck him and his close-minded bigotry."

The resulting clang caused Holly to jump.

She'd been right about Trent. He wasn't the kind of guy she could fall for.

Not even in lust. Not even for a night.

"Look, there's obviously a lot going on here that I know nothing about." Holly distanced herself from Trent as one of the nurses motioned to the security guard in the lobby. "Your roommates should be here soon. Why don't I wait outside for them?"

Trent hung his head, his fists balling. The heaving of his back kept her from doing as she'd suggested, though. No matter what he claimed, he'd been stabbed straight through the heart, either by his father's death or whatever it was that would forever be left unfinished between them.

Shit.

Holly took a tentative step closer then another, her fancy heels out of place as they clicked against the institutional linoleum. She put her hand on his shoulder, but he shrugged it off. "I'll be right by the door if you need some air."

He jerked his head once in acknowledgement but didn't go with her as she headed for the exit, hugging her churning stomach. Now she wished she hadn't eaten so much of the rich offerings at Kari's engagement party or shaken herself up with so much dancing—and making out, after.

She'd barely emerged into the neon night when the limo screeched to a halt under the emergency room portico. Andi was the first out, crossing to her and crushing her in a bear hug. "Where's Trent? What's happening?"

To her surprise, he was only a few steps behind. He'd followed her after all. "My father is dead. Sorry to ruin your party. Let's go back."

"What?" Ford asked, as if he had to have heard wrong.

Holly realized she was shivering when Andi rubbed her hands up and down Holly's arms. Nothing could quite warm her after what she'd seen inside. None of it made any sense, but suddenly all she wanted to do was go home and spend time with her mom.

Until Cooper spoke up. "I'm so sorry, Trent. I know things weren't good between you guys, but that still has to hurt. Are you sure you don't want to go in and spend time with your family?"

"They don't want me here. It was the last thing my father commanded. To keep me out." Trent cursed. Worse than his bitterness was the monotone voice he used. No one deserved that kind of treatment, especially not from their blood.

"That's bullshit," Simon added, punching his palm. "You guys are lawyers, isn't there anything we can do? Doesn't Trent have some kind of rights?"

Ford, Brady, and Josh looked to Cooper, who obviously knew more about what was going on but was also a junior lawyer in their firm. He shook his head. "Unfortunately, not tonight. If his dad communicated his wishes to the staff, they will honor them. Still, that doesn't mean we can't help."

"Why don't we go back to the hotel and figure something out?" Brady suggested.

"That's very generous, but I'm sure that's not how you planned to spend the rest of your night." Trent scrunched his eyes closed. "I think I'm just going to go home so the rest of you can have fun. Sorry to ruin everything you set up."

"You didn't mess up anything," Kari promised, her eyes still misty as she glanced at the humongous gleaming diamond on her ring finger. "I love these guys because of who they are, and the men they are don't let their friends suffer alone. Come on, please."

She gestured toward the open limo door. Trent looked at it, his current roommates, then at his five college friends, and last at the people they'd somehow all become involved with. It was crazy how life worked sometimes, taking away the family you were born with and replacing it with one you built yourself.

For the first time since her mom had been diagnosed as terminal, Holly thought maybe there was hope that she wouldn't end up alone.

If she could give Trent even a fraction of that same comfort, especially when he needed it most, she was in. "Do you mind if I come too?"

He looked back and extended his hand. "I wasn't going to ask, but yeah...I'd really appreciate that."

Andi and Kari exchanged a very unsubtle look that Holly assumed would have been a full-fledged high-five if the circumstances had been different.

When she crouched and entered the limo, her spike heel got caught in the crack of a paver, sending her tumbling onto Trent's lap. His arm was around her waist, holding her to him instead of shoving her away before she could right herself. Even in the limo there wasn't quite enough room for all of them, so she didn't object to staying there for the remainder of the ride.

Holly let herself pretend she did it to comfort Trent, when really she was the one finding solace in the life lessons she'd been taught in the few short hours since she'd reconnected with him.

She was hardly a mile from her home, and yet it seemed like she'd come so far from where she'd been, locked inside, focused on only the negative parts of her existence just a few short hours ago.

If her mother could see her then and read her thoughts, she would be even happier than when Holly had sent that selfie of herself, flawlessly coifed.

Things might not be perfect, but that was life, and with friends like these by her side, she might be able to handle the difficult things that were ahead.

7

Trent used his thumbs to massage his temples but it didn't alleviate the pounding there.

He probably should lay off the expensive whiskey that Josh kept offering him, but no one blamed him for needing a few stiff drinks to get through the night. Of course, he should have known it had started out entirely too promising to wind up the same way.

He cast a stare over at Holly, who had curled up beside him on a couch more comfortable than his bed. She'd kicked off her heels and tucked her feet beneath her, making her look like a powerful panther in her sexy black dress instead of the cute kitten he'd once thought of her as. Maybe, just as his family had done to him, he'd underestimated her.

He wouldn't make that mistake again.

She sipped a fruity peach drink from a fancy glass that someone had snagged from the engagement party that still raged down the hall despite the departure of the guests of honor.

Cooper was on his cell, talking to someone while tapping away at the keyboard of his laptop, which he'd set up on the glossy surface of a desk in the ornate suite his bosses had rented to woo their soon-to-be wife. And instead, here they were, trying to clean up his mess.

If Trent thought they'd listen, he would have objected, offered to leave for the one-millionth time since they'd returned from the hospital. It had taken a few hours for them to call in favors from their connections, a few of whom were in attendance at the party.

Most people probably thought they were celebrating in private instead of trying to figure out a way for Trent to reconcile with his family, at least long enough to get some closure. Of course, there was one easy path...to denounce who he was and what he wanted, but looking around the room at the complex bonds between his friends and their friends, he could never say with a straight face that he thought what they were doing was wrong.

Or that he wasn't jealous as hell that he didn't have something similar for himself.

"Are you saying what I think you're saying?" Cooper's voice rose along with his eyebrows. He glanced at Trent, then began to type furiously, taking notes. "Yeah. I just got the email. I'm going to review the documents. Can I call you back if we have additional questions?"

A pause hung in the air, everyone being still and quiet at once, which was kind of a miracle. "Thanks so much. You've been a huge help. Yes, Westford, Arman, and King will be representing Trent in this matter going forward."

They would be? Trent took another sip of whiskey. He was pretty sure he couldn't afford a team as qualified and competent as them without digging into his savings for his business. He stood, crossing to Cooper and squeezing his shoulder. "I appreciate your help, really I do. But that's not necessary. I can figure this out on my own."

"No, I don't think you can." Cooper swiveled his chair toward Ford, Brady, and Josh, who were waiting for a debriefing. It was easy to imagine them ruling a boardroom or a courtroom as they focused their combined attention on their staff member. "There's a trust with some very specific stipulations in here."

"How big of a fucking disaster did he leave me?" Trent groaned.

"It's complicated," Cooper said as he flipped through the electronic documents in front of him. "But...at a first glance...it looks like it's going to be *very* worth your while to get this sorted out. And fast."

"I didn't give a shit about my father's money when he was alive, why would I want it now?" Trent sliced his hands through the air, wishing he could cut off the pain his father could cause him, even from the grave. "What do I have to do, promise I'll be *normal* and leave my wicked ways behind me?"

"Kind of." Ford nodded as he peeked over Cooper's shoulder. "You'd have to be married or over twenty-five to inherit what he's set aside for you."

"So that bastard thought poly was some kind of phase I'd grow out of? Fuck him!" Trent wasn't a violent sort of guy, but he wished he could chuck his glass across the room and relish it shattering. He didn't need distractions. All he had to do was put his head down, work hard, and focus on his goals to achieve them. "Why are we wasting our breath talking about this when I could be downstairs on the casino floor making more money to start my business myself?"

It just might take a while, time his competitors could

use to reverse engineer his technology if they caught even a hint of what he'd dreamed up. Several players in the industry were close on his heels, with enormous budgets and full research and development teams. Worry that they would catch up or pass him ate at him every day.

"Why couldn't he have held on another three damn months? I'll be twenty-five in June."

"How much money do you need to fund your patents and the start-up costs for your solar and battery technology?" Cooper asked.

"Too much." Trent squeezed the bridge of his nose. "I might be too late to market by the time I have it."

"Whoa, is that the business Lorenzo was referring to earlier?" Brady asked. "That could be a big fucking deal."

Owen and Lorenzo were staring at him with twin worried gazes. They knew how much this meant to him and how deeply his family could fuck him up on a personal level, and now on a professional one, too.

"It *will* be." Trent crossed his arms. "When I do it. On my own. Without my father's dirty money and sacrificing things I can't live without. I'm not going to change who I am. Not even for this."

"Hold on." Holly put her feet on the floor and leaned forward. "No one's saying you have to actually change. Just do what it takes to meet the trust's qualifications."

Trent scoffed. "Oh yeah, where am I going to find some random woman to marry me tonight? Are you volunteering?"

Though he'd said it to prove a point, he couldn't deny that part of him didn't hate that idea as much as he should.

Holly blinked a few times in rapid succession then sat

back, her mouth snapping shut. Yeah, that's what he'd thought.

Everyone else surrounding them was so quiet he could sense the faint thump of the bass through the soundproofed walls.

"Guys, that's not the worst idea I've ever heard." Owen spread his arms. "Maybe you should think about it."

"Exactly how much money are we talking about here?" Holly asked.

Cooper squinted, then said, "After taxes and legal fees, I'm guessing seventy, give or take."

"Seventy thousand dollars?" Holly's eyes went wide. "Trent, you could do a lot with that. It would be a huge head start on your dreams."

She was sweet, and entirely too naive for the sort of bullshit their well-meaning friends were trying to entangle her in.

Josh sidled up next to Ford and glanced between Holly and the screen twice, as if to make certain of what he'd read. Then he whistled. "Not thousands, Holly. *Millions.*"

The drink nearly slipped from her fingers, but Andi was there to catch it and set it on the table beside the couch. Holly's pretty eyes nearly popped out of her head. "Millions? Of dollars?"

Trent cursed. He'd resisted temptation once in his life already. Could he do it again, now that he knew the stakes? What if he didn't do this and someone beat him to finalizing the revolutionary solar technology he was on the cusp of perfecting?

All he had to do was get hitched for ninety days, and he'd have a shot to realize his dreams. Besides, assuming she would even go for it, he'd get to spend more time with

Holly while he took the next step toward his goal. Maybe it was the whiskey talking, or the eager expressions on his friends' faces, but he was finding it hard to remember why this was a terrible plan.

Thinking out loud, he said to Holly, "I'd make it worth your while too if we did this."

Andi clapped and Kari grinned. Lorenzo slapped Owen on the back and they both shot him approving glances. Of course they did. Because if he did this stupid, reckless thing, that meant Holly would be living with them for three months too. And there was only one way that was going to end up. The chemistry had been there earlier. It would be again.

She had no idea what she was getting herself into.

"Hold on. You're saying that you'd pay me to marry you?" Holly snatched her drink up again and drained it dry. She stood, and he wondered if she was about to smack him, except she paused halfway across the plush carpet between them. Her eyes shifted out the window, as if she was thinking of something far away... "How much?"

"What?" He whirled around to gawk like she had grown an extra head. She couldn't be considering such a ridiculous charade. Could she?

"How. Much?"

"What would you want to do it?" Trent asked. "It's just for ninety days or so until I turn twenty-five. Then we could get it annulled, right?"

He aimed that last question at the quartet of lawyers in the room.

Ford was skimming the documents over Cooper's shoulder and they both nodded. "Yes. It just says you need to be married or over the age of twenty-five to claim the funds and keep them from rolling into the general estate. There's no stipulation on how long you have to have been hitched or who you need to be with. I guess your dad figured if you'd settled down…"

"Well, he thought wrong." Trent tried not to yell at them. They weren't the ones discriminating against him. "So, Holly, what would it take?"

He knew he was being kind of an asshole, but he didn't think she'd consider it for any amount of money and it pissed him off that he was even entertaining the thought, never mind kind of starting to like it.

So it shocked him when she fired right back at him. "Four hundred thirty-seven thousand, two hundred eighty-one dollars, and seventeen cents."

Trent threw back his head and laughed.

Holly didn't.

"Wait, that wasn't a joke?"

"Do I look like I'm kidding?" Her cheeks reddened, and he realized he'd almost blown things before they'd really started getting serious.

"No, it's just that's oddly specific." Trent cocked his head. "What do you need it for?"

"Is the deal contingent on what I'm going to do with the money?" She propped her hands on her hips. He felt his chances with both her and his dad's stupid will slipping away.

"Not at all." He held his hands up, palms out. "I'm curious, that's all."

Holly sighed. "That's apparently the going rate for a kidney transplant in the US these days if you don't have health insurance."

"Holy shit." Cooper whistled.

Trent's stomach soured. It had nothing to do with the slightly too much he'd had to drink. He felt more scared than when his father had been in that hospital taking his last breaths, which only made him feel sicker for being such an unfeeling asshole. "Are you ill?"

Holly wilted. She shook her head and inched closer to him. "Not me. My mom. She has lupus. I've been taking care of her these past couple of years. My father died of mesothelioma triggered by his work and she gets about twenty grand a year from the settlement. That's enough to disqualify her from Medicaid but not enough for us to afford market insurance. Hell, we can barely scrape up the minimum payments for her dialysis treatments. Now she's getting worse. She has a spot at the top of the transplant list, but until we can prove we have the funds for the anti-rejection drugs, they won't clear her because it would be a waste of a precious organ, and without this surgery..."

She gulped.

Trent didn't hesitate; he crossed the gap between them and wrapped her in his arms. "I'm so sorry, Holly."

"You're the one who lost your dad tonight. You shouldn't be comforting me." Still, she didn't pull away. Instead, she hugged him back and they stood there, rocking slightly, in each other's arms.

When he looked up, everyone in the room was smiling, except for Kari, who knuckled a tear from the corner of her eye. Right then, Trent knew he was going to do it. If not for himself, then for Holly. And her mom. It was literally a matter of life and death. And if they stuck it to his dad in the process, well, more the better.

"Ford, can you guys put something in writing? Make our deal official?" Trent never took his stare off Holly. "Give her enough to cover the transplant and in-home care for her mom, since she's going to have to stay with me, Lorenzo, and Owen."

"Wait, what?" Holly blanched.

"You can't expect people to believe we're married if you're still living at home. And I don't think there's enough room for your mom to be comfortable at our place." He closed his eyes. "But if that's a deal breaker, I understand."

Holly searched his stare, as if trying to find the answers to questions they both had and didn't understand. Finally she said, "It's not. If I don't do this, she won't have any shot. I can stay by her side and watch her fade away, or do this temporarily to give her some real quality time. She'll be better off without me in the short-term."

Trent tucked an errant lock of hair behind her ear and cupped her cheek. "She's lucky to have you. And so am I. We can go over for dinner there every night if you want."

"I do." She chuckled at her own choice of words. Holly cut her stare to Ford and said, "Go ahead, draw it up, please. Before I come to my senses."

"I mean...we'll have to be a bit creative in how we word things, but sure." He rubbed his hands together. "We can make this happen."

Holly glanced over her shoulder at Andi and Kari, both of whom beamed at them.

Trent did the same, looking to Owen and Lorenzo for validation that he hadn't lost his fucking mind. They both flashed him a thumbs-up along with a sinful grin that meant they were hoping for more than a fourth platonic roommate.

Trent couldn't even think that far ahead at the moment, though his body certainly approved of keeping

Holly tucked close to him right then, as well as during the following ninety days.

When they returned their stares to each other, something intense and hot passed between them. A combined purpose, a dedication to their goals no matter the cost, and—just maybe—a shower of sparks caused by their mutual attraction.

"Well then, who wants to come to our wedding?" Holly asked.

A chorus of agreement echoed around them. It had been so long since Trent had that kind of unqualified acceptance that a rush of elation ran through him. Before he could feel guilty about it given the circumstances, he shared the moment with Holly.

Trent lowered his head and sealed their agreement with a smoking kiss that guaranteed they were going to take up right where they'd left off at the party earlier once they were alone again. Someone whistled while a few other people hooted and a round of applause erupted.

The chaos was the only thing that jarred him from the moment and reminded him that this wasn't the time or place to lose control. Trent lifted his lips just enough to break the spell and stood there breathing hard while Holly steadied herself.

She squeezed his arms before letting go and stepping back, but he didn't let her get far. He took her hand in his and joked, "Can Elvis officiate?"

"Hell, yes. The more fun, the better." Holly grinned. Maybe because continuing their party atmosphere was the only way either of them was going to have the nerve to go through with what they were about to do.

"Dibs on maid of honor!" Andi shouted before bouncing up and down.

That led to Lorenzo and Owen arm wrestling to determine who would be best man. Holly and Trent laughed at their friends' antics. He'd never felt as lucky or as normal as he did in those very unusual and twisted circumstances.

8

"I didn't even know you were going to get engaged tonight, never mind that I'd be getting married." Holly blinked at the slightly worn silk bouquet in her hands before glancing up at her two best friends. Their guys mingled nearby, laughing and making the most of their second detour from the engagement party while Trent finished up some paperwork in the front office. The documents that would make their union official. "How the hell did we end up here?"

Oh yeah. She'd followed a trail of golden breadcrumbs right to the chapel door.

$437,281.17

That's how they'd lured her into a cheesy chapel on the strip with a guy she'd snuck longing glances at out her bedroom window for a few years in college. Just like his killer smile, that amount had been burned into her brain. The number of times she'd withdrawn the estimate from the envelope and stared at it in horror, weeping over the impossibility of raising that much cash in her lifetime, never mind her mother's, guaranteed she knew it by heart.

That was why she was doing this. And if she was attracted to her soon-to-be husband, well, that only made things more bearable, right? She could put up with anything for ninety days if it meant she could give her mother the one thing she needed to be healthy. Hell, she'd have gladly given her mom her own kidney if she'd been a match.

Kari glanced down at the honking rock that covered her ring finger from the second to third knuckle. Surrounded by sapphires and emeralds, it reminded Holly of something a mermaid queen would wear. The lawyers did have a thing for the ocean, and even owned an enormous sailing yacht. It fit her perfectly and looked gorgeous, but the ring highlighted the difference between her friends' true love story, and the mutually beneficial arrangement she'd made with Trent.

Was she about to make the worst mistake of her life?

"Would you feel better if we turned this into a double date?" Kari asked Holly. "Maybe me, Ford, Brady, and Josh should make it official...well, as official as we can...while we're here."

"Seriously? You would do that?" Holly wasn't sure why that caught her off-guard. The thought of someone else being as impulsive as her did help. Hell, Kari would be signing up for a lifetime commitment, not just a ninety-day trial period.

"We're here. We're together. Elvis is in the building. Why not?" As Kari asked the question, she looked not at Holly but at her trio of sexy men, who perked up at the suggestion.

"You don't want something fancy and extravagant?" Josh asked, though the tone of his question made it clear he was not-so-secretly optimistic at the news.

"All the important stuff is here." She looked at each of the men. "And now that you've proposed, I don't want to wait. We can do the official deed now and have some kind of party for everyone else back home. You know, with the pretty dress and good food and shit. If that's what you want."

"That sounds perfect." Ford nodded.

"Let's do it," Brady added.

"I don't want to say so in front of Trent, but this really is going to be the best night of my life." Ford crushed Kari in a hug so tight it made her squeak while her toes lifted off the ground. And when he set her back down, he stole a quick kiss before a frown marred his elated expression.

"What?" She asked.

"We can't all marry you. Technically." He looked over his shoulder to his partners. "Which one of us do you want to be on the marriage license?"

Kari shook her head. "I'm not going to choose between you. I love you equally, you know that."

"Guess we'll have to rock-paper-scissors it." Josh shrugged.

"You're going to leave something that important to chance?" Holly was horrified. All her life she'd been a planner. Someone who mapped things out and worked toward her objectives with relentless determination.

Kari laughed. "Sure, why not?"

"There might be advantages to each of you from picking one or the other. Benefits, life insurance stuff, I don't know. It would be irrational to choose on a whim." She tried to get them to see reason.

"No offense, Holly..." Reed jumped in to defend his friends. "You can't control everything in life. Look at us. None of us imagined this is where we'd be today, or any day, and I've never been happier. It's great to have goals and to try to imagine every possible outcome of our decisions and what you'd do if they came to pass, but sometimes you just have to ride the wave and see where it takes you."

The butterflies in her stomach calmed some as she realized he was exactly right. She was never going to get another chance like this. So she had to grab the gold wedding ring while she could.

Andi hugged her. "He's smart, that husband of mine. You're doing the right thing. Who knows, maybe you'll want to stay married after the ninety days are up."

That was almost a scarier thought.

What if she fell for Trent and all he wanted was a way to access his father's cash? She'd have to make sure she guarded her heart because it would be too easy to imagine he gave a shit when he was only being his usual, charismatic self.

The way his best friends had rallied around, including her in their conversations, joking with her about Trent's bad habits, and promising that by marrying their roommate she was getting a three-for-one deal, with them to look out for her and help her with anything she needed while she was staying with them... Well, that wasn't going to make her any less likely to become too comfortable in her temporary home.

She glanced up in time to catch Lorenzo and Owen eying her with a blend of curiosity and barely veiled hunger but by no means objecting to Andi's overreach.

"I got it." Trent waved the paperwork over his head as he joined them in the chapel. He wasn't smiling as he approached her, his face stony and determined. He stopped directly in front of her. "Last chance to change your mind. Are you sure you want to go through with this?"

It wasn't even a choice. Her mother needed this. She was doing it. "Absolutely. You?"

Trent hesitated, making Holly's knees go weak. What if he backed out now?

Holly put her hand over his, which clasped the license hard enough to crumple it on the edge. "It's going to be okay, Trent. I'll be in this with you."

"I know. Thank you." He lowered his voice and stepped closer. "It's just that I've been working hard to do this without my father's money. Am I going to regret taking this path later?"

Holly squeezed his fingers. "There's nothing wrong with pursuing your dreams however you have to get there. You're going to change the world. Make life better for millions of people. That's worth it. And when you're rich and famous, you can set up a scholarship fund for people like you to do the same."

Trent nodded slowly, as if he was really considering everything she had to say. "You're right, Holly. Let's do this. For you, for me, for your mom, and the future."

"For the future." It seemed natural to go up on her tiptoes and kiss him. While she only meant it to be a friendly peck, it appeared they weren't capable of keeping things sweet between them. His arms came around her and he held her close as his lips slid over hers in a seductive promise.

She wondered if their unconventional wedding would end in a traditional wedding night.

It wouldn't be the worst thing to ever happen to her.

Their friends cheered and whistled. Until Elvis

entered, and joked, "Hey, usually we save that part for last. Is everyone ready?"

When Holly and Trent broke apart, his frown had been replaced with a wide smile, aimed right at her. It might not be her usual style, but it was obvious that she'd already taken this leap with him.

Kari spoke up. "We'd like to join too. Me and..."

Holly turned toward the lawyers in time to see Ford, Brady, and Josh wrapping up the best out of three. Ford's rock smashed Brady and Josh's scissors. He whooped. "That's right, I'm getting married, suckers!"

The officiant shook his head. "I've seen some crazy things before, but I admit, that's a new one. Why don't we do the ceremony first and then you can sort out your papers afterward to make it official?"

"Perfect." Ford grinned. "I can't wait another moment to make Kari our wife."

Brady and Josh each put a hand on his shoulders and congratulated him. It didn't matter what was written for the records. They were equals in their relationship with Kari, their friendship, and even their law firm.

As they approached the front of the chapel, Owen and Lorenzo flanked Trent much like Brady and Josh did to Ford. Holly knew it was only because they were his friends and the witnesses for their ceremony, but she would have been lying if it didn't make her wonder, for just a few moments, what it would be like to be loved by one man, or by three like Kari and Andi.

Holly couldn't say she paid much attention to their actual wedding ceremony, which only lasted about five minutes. But she would remember every detail of Trent's face during that time. His eyes were locked with hers, filled with sadness, hope, excitement, and sympathy. You can learn a lot from staring at someone that long, and as the seconds passed, she was sure she could see straight to his soul.

Surprisingly, it didn't look that different than her own.

He had ambitions. He had problems. And he was doing his best to thrive despite them. She vowed then and there to do the same.

Holly was doing this for her mom. But maybe she also needed to do it for herself.

"Who has the rings?" Elvis asked.

"We don't have—" Holly shook her head but stopped explaining when Trent cut her off.

"I do." He fished in his pocket and pulled two plain gold bands—one about twice as thick as the other—from inside. He held out his hand, with them touching in his palm. Simple, classic, and so damn sweet that Holly felt her eyes prickle. "I know this can't be what you had in mind for your wedding day, but I hope you'll take this as a promise from me that I plan to make the most of our time together."

"Awww." Andi fanned her face from her post in the front row.

He slipped the ring onto her finger, twisting it a smidge to seat it fully.

The weight of the symbol felt new and didn't freak her out in the least. How could it when he was being such a gentleman about the whole situation? She plucked the heavier ring from his hand and held it out as she said, "It's really you I have to thank for asking me to marry you and changing my life, and my family's life for the better. You literally saved us. Thank you. For whatever time we have together, I will be the best damn wife you could have hoped for."

Holly winked at him as she put the ring on his finger, liking the way it looked against his tanned skin.

"Damn, they're making us look bad," Josh bitched as Kari knuckled a tear from the corner of her eye. "Brady, you're the one good at this shit. Say something romantic and profound."

"I don't have the words to say everything I feel, so I have to hope that you already know." Brady looked not only at Kari, but at Ford and Josh as well. "The best I can do is to say I love you and I love what we share. As long as I'm alive, none of you will be alone."

"Oh. That was perfect." Andi leaned against Cooper, rested her head on Reed's shoulder and clasped Simon's hand. Holly couldn't even be jealous because she was looking at Trent, who was still holding her gaze. At least until he glanced at his roommates, both of whom were grinning.

Elvis cleared his throat, then said, "I declare you...married."

When he didn't finish soon enough, Josh said, "Now we get to kiss, right?"

"Go for it." The man nodded.

Holly was beaming as Trent swooped in and picked up where they'd left off before the ceremony. It had only been a few minutes, but she'd missed the feel of him so close, his heat seeping into her as he swept his lips over hers.

"Come on, let's go back and celebrate properly. It can be both our engagement party and our first wedding reception." Ford waved toward the limo, which was still waiting out front. With one last nip on her lower lip, Trent started to join them.

Holly slowed down, dragging Trent with her since their hands were still linked.

"You okay?" he asked.

"Would you mind if we didn't go back?" She had wanted to leave hours ago and spend some quality time with him. Everything that had happened since hadn't changed that desire. Even if they just sat quietly and processed everything that had gone on, she'd be more up for that than loud music, booze, and dancing.

Their friends, including Owen and Lorenzo, were already piling into the car. A cork flew out the open sunroof as they popped some champagne. A chorus of cheers radiated from the limo.

Trent looked from the car to her and smiled. "I'm so glad you said that. Hang on, I'll let them know."

He jogged over to the limo, then leaned inside. After a few seconds, Andi poked her head out the door and said, "Congratulations! Good night! Call me tomorrow and tell me everything!"

Holly waved and met Trent halfway. He looped his arm around her as the gang rolled away from the curb, leaving them in the glow of Vegas's neon lights. "Ready to go home?"

Home.

She thought of her mother and the apartment they shared. It was a place to live, but it wasn't what she considered a home. Would Trent's place be any better? Holly was willing to give it a try; she just couldn't let herself forget it was temporary.

"Can I take you somewhere?" a man called from down the street. When Holly glanced up, she realized it was an operator with a horse-drawn carriage.

Trent looked at her and laughed. "Hey, why not?"

Holly grinned. She couldn't deny the thought of snuggling up to him in the romantic ride while looking at her shiny new ring made her feel a lot better about what they'd done, even aside from the money. He boosted her into the carriage, then took the seat next to her, giving the driver directions to his place, which wasn't very far away.

"Help yourself to some drinks," the man suggested as he steered them into the road.

Trent took a pitcher of something fruity and bubbly and poured them each a flute before handing her one.

Holly held it up and made a toast. "Here's to getting what you need."

"I'd rather toast to getting what you want." Trent clinked his glass with hers. "Maybe we can figure out how to do both."

Warmth—and not only from the alcohol she'd imbibed across the night, the effects of which were amplified by her riot of emotions and lack of sleep—spread through Holly. Her toes curled when Trent sipped from her lips and the sound of the horse's hooves on the pavement made a steady rhythm for them to make out to. Already she'd gotten used to the way they came together, how natural and seamless it was.

And she wanted to spend what few hours were left in the night doing it over and over.

9

———

The world spun as Trent swept her off her feet, literally. He swung her into his arms and carried her from their ride, across the threshold, and into the house he shared with Lorenzo and Owen. It was too dark for her to see much, but from what she could tell it was modest and well maintained.

And given the direction they'd traveled from the strip, it couldn't be more than a mile from the apartment she'd been existing in with her mother for the past few years. Son of a bitch.

He and his hot friends had been here the whole time, just like college all over again.

Well, tonight she didn't plan to waste the chance to finally be in the same house, and same bed, as him. Hopefully he was planning to consummate their faux-marriage with very real orgasms, like she was.

Of course she'd understand if shock, grief, or even pure exhaustion prevented them from acting on the wild magnetism drawing them together. None of that seemed to be slowing him, though.

Instead of setting her down in the living room, Trent marched straight to what she assumed was his room. He lowered her to the floor and kept a hand on her waist when the world kept wobbling just a little. She might have had one too many glasses of peach champagne on the way there. It wasn't every day she planned to seduce someone, never mind her newly wedded husband.

Was Trent thinking the same thing? His hand rubbed up to her ribs then back along her sequined dress, almost onto her ass.

"I never thought my bride would wear black." Trent shrugged. "Well, okay, I never imagined I'd get married, but I wouldn't blame you if you're sad about it. I promise it'll just be for a few months and then we can forget this ever happened."

Holly wasn't sure why that thought didn't reassure her much.

She might have needed one more celebration drink to overcome her inhibitions and say what she was really thinking....what she really wanted. But that wasn't an option now, so she imagined what her friends would say if they were there.

Don't miss out on this opportunity! We saw the way he looked at you before, and how he was making out with you. There's chemistry there and you're both adults. Do it before it's too late.

"Is this where I'm going to be sleeping?" she asked.

"This is my bed." He waved toward the soft, rumpled gray duvet, which did look pretty damn comfortable. "You heard what Cooper and the rest of the lawyers said. It has to look...no, *be* real. Especially given the timing of our nuptials, I'm guessing someone's going to investigate our marriage to vet it."

Holly bit her lower lip. It might be the perfect excuse to take what she wanted but never otherwise would have had the guts to go for. She nodded. "Okay, then. Let's do this."

She took the hem of her dress in her hands and began to shimmy it up her body, revealing the sexy lingerie she'd worn mostly to humor her friends. Thank God they were more worldly and smarter than her, because they had to have guessed it might pay off.

"Whoa. What are you doing?" Trent asked, putting his hand over his face, though his fingers split, allowing him to peek through them at her curves.

"Getting undressed. You can't expect me to sleep in these clothes."

He nodded. "Yeah. Sorry. Let me get you a T-shirt or something."

"I don't want one." She let the dress drop to the floor and stood before him in only black lace and extra-tall heels. She allowed herself to become his wife, shedding the young woman who'd been dragged to a party by her friends like she did the fancy clothes.

"You like to sleep naked?" he asked with a gulp.

It might have been funny if she wasn't so artless. Instead of the gentleman he was being, she wanted the man from the bushes.

She shook her head no. "Not usually, but on my wedding night it seems like it would be advantageous."

"You're saying you want to sleep with me?" he asked point blank.

"I'm hoping we won't be sleeping for a while." She nodded and approached him. "You said it yourself. This has to be real. We're married, and that's what husbands and wives do, especially on their wedding night. Let's consummate this bitch."

"I'm not paying you for sex." He held her at arm's length, his elbows locked as if to keep him from caving to temptation.

"Nope. But if we do it anyway, then it will only help things, not hurt, right?" Holly didn't want him to be logical or chivalrous now. She needed him, damn it. It was the one selfish benefit she might get from their arrangement, and she intended to take it.

But maybe that was callous given the night they'd had and how drastically his world had changed. Maybe he wasn't into it, or her, after everything that had happened. Holly paused, staring up at him, reading the conflicting emotions in his gorgeous blue eyes. "No pressure. I get that tonight was...a lot. It seemed, though, like you might still be interested in seeing where we were about to end up after you finished ravishing me behind that potted palm."

"I don't know why what you're saying is starting to make sense." He shook his head. "I should know better. Except it's been a hell of a night, and losing myself in you sounds like heaven. Look, maybe I just need this...need *you*, right now."

Funny how she'd thought the same thing. Holly hoped she could make them both feel better. She held her arms out. "Then come and get me."

Trent's mouth bent from a frown to a naughty smile, then he lunged, putting her over his shoulder. His hand landed on her ass a little harder than necessary to keep her stable as she dangled over his back. Oh yeah, gentle Trent was gone and his rakish twin had taken over.

Thank God.

"Did you just spank me?" she asked with a laugh.

"Why? Did you like it?"

Her legs shifted, her thighs brushing together as she realized she had. A little too much.

"Maybe," she answered honestly as he laid her gently on the bed.

"Hmm." He undid his belt, making her shiver. "We'll come back to that. Later. Or some other time. Once I can read you better and understand your desires. Tonight, I want to be boring. Pretend that I'm normal, and enjoy the simple pleasure of making love to you for the first time. Is that okay with you?"

"Uh huh." Holly nodded, reaching for him as he finished discarding his clothes. The six-pack he'd hidden under his navy button-down shirt begged her to touch him, to test the muscles flexing as he climbed into bed beside her.

Of course, her stare dipped between his legs. If she hadn't been sure before, there was no mistaking his desire for her now. Trent was ready and more than capable of bringing her dirtiest dreams to life.

He didn't rush, though, not even knowing she was a guaranteed thing. Instead, he ran his fingers along the edges of each piece of lace and silk wrapping her body like a present intended only for him. He brushed the pad of his thumb over her nipples, which were hard and clearly visible through the sheer material.

"It's a shame to take this off of you." He kissed her chest between the panels of the lingerie. "You're gorgeous, Holly."

"You can thank Andi and Kari. They did all this." She

winced. "I'm still the same boring girl next door when I'm not going to billionaires' engagement parties. Sorry."

He nipped her shoulder and growled. "I happen to like that Holly a lot. Never apologize for who you are. If it takes me the next eighty-nine nights to prove it to you, I guess we're going to be spending a lot of time in here together."

"Not complaining," she murmured.

He chuckled at that, seeming truly amused by her awkward sense of humor. "Relax, Holly. I'm not going to bite unless you want me to." His hands ran down her arms then all the way along her middle fingers. Her toes curled, making her realize she still had her heels on.

Not for long, as Trent scooted lower, caressing her thighs then her calves until he slipped the shoes from her feet and placed them lovingly on the ground. "Those make your legs and ass look even more incredible than I already knew they were."

"Oh yeah?"

"Yeah." He crawled up her body, settling between her legs, then whispered against her mouth, "You wore jeans better than any woman on campus. I might have stared at you getting in Andi's car a time or thirty from my window. Sorry, kind of...but not really."

Holly hugged him with her knees against his hips. The weight of his cock on her mound made it impossible for her to call him a liar. And when he kissed her, with a little more spice than he had in the penthouse earlier, she believed him.

Trent kissed along her jaw then down her neck, eliciting a sigh. "Remember that time I told you I went to your swim meet to cheer on my lab partner?"

He hesitated and looked up at her. "Uh huh."

"The only person I knew there was you." She put her hand over her face, embarrassed, even now, to admit that she'd gone there to ogle his near-perfect physique and had stayed to cheer him to victory.

Trent's smile expanded, and he returned to her mouth, spending an inordinate amount of time sipping from her lips and teasing her with swirls of his tongue against her own.

She lost track of everything but how he made her feel and reacting to it in a way that enhanced both of their pleasure. While he was kissing her, his hands wandered, finding the ties and hooks that kept her lingerie in place before systematically unfastening them one by one.

When he peeled it away and left her bare before him, she didn't even flinch, because his gaze held so much admiration and lust, there was nothing to be ashamed or embarrassed of about her imperfect body. Without a word, he increased her confidence and made her feel like she was worth more than the trust fund he was about to inherit.

Trent lowered his head and took her breast into his mouth while his hand massaged the other. He used his knee to press against her core, until she arched, panting against him, holding nothing back.

How could she when he did such amazing things to her?

Holly reached for him, running her hands down his back and squeezing his ass, her freshly manicured nails digging in slightly as she tried to bring him closer, where she wanted him most.

He resisted, making several more circuits across her breasts, stomach, and lower before he caved. She wondered if it was possible to come from foreplay alone. Probably not, but if she could grind on him a little more…

Trent pinched her nipple, just enough to get her attention. "You're ready to come?"

"I was ready like an hour ago." She couldn't help being impatient when he'd strung things out so long. Her desire obliterated the filter between her libido and her mouth. "Please, Trent. Fuck me."

He hummed, his eyes narrowing, but he didn't give in despite the thick bead of precome rolling down his shaft. "Soon. Ish. Soonish."

He grinned and snaked down her body until his face was hovering above her mound.

Thinking of how he'd kissed her and how that same talented mouth was about to be working her pussy, she nearly came before he'd had a chance to blow her mind. Almost, but not quite.

Trent ate her as if she was more of a delicacy than the food they'd shared at Kari's party.

He took his time, savoring every nibble, lick, and suck. And when he concentrated his efforts on her clit, she moaned.

The encouraging hum he made in response, sending vibrations through her sensitive flesh, set her off. An orgasm rushed through her, making her flood his mouth with her arousal. As if the first flush of passion only inspired him more, Trent buried his face in her core and devoured her, making her come several more times in rapid succession.

"Holy shit. I didn't even know that was possible." She gasped as she clutched his bedspread to keep from flying into space as he launched her higher and higher.

"That's a damn shame," he growled against her skin. "I

should have showed you before. And we haven't even gotten to the good part yet."

Holly didn't want to argue, not when he was lavishing such pleasure on her. But she couldn't imagine anything being better than what he'd already done to her, over and over.

She still wanted to be joined with him, to be that close, and share the experience even if she expected it to be more for his benefit than hers. So she hooked her hands under his arms and tugged until he got the point and rose over her, aligning their bodies.

"I need to go get a condom. They're in Lorenzo's room. We don't usually..." He cleared his throat.

"What?" She swiped her thumb over his lower lip, which was swollen from pleasuring her. He had nothing to hide from her.

"I've never had sex with a woman in my room before. When we're together, it's usually in his room or the living room."

Right out in the open? Holly shivered at the thought. But when he moved to leave, she clutched him to her. "Don't go. I mean, I'm on birth control. And I've been tested. If you have too, there's no reason we need protection."

"I have." Trent stared up at the ceiling as if praying for control. "You're saying I can come inside you? Bare?"

"If you want." She nodded, wondering if that was too much too soon. But here he was, about to enter her and she didn't want anything between them. Not the rules of their stupid agreement or his insecurities about his sexuality or any physical barrier either.

"I want, Holly, I do. I'm sorry you never knew how badly I wanted to do this before," he whispered in her ear before the tip of his cock nudged her opening. "Believe me, I spent plenty of nights in my bed not too far from yours imagining exactly what this would feel like while I...well..."

"You masturbated to the thought of sleeping with me?" Holly's eyes opened wide.

"Uh, yeah." He advanced a bit, notching the head of his cock in her pussy.

Holly moaned. "Good. That makes me feel like less of a perv for doing the same while thinking of you. Damn you, I couldn't get the thought of you fucking that girl in the bushes out of my head for years."

"It's only been a couple years now, Holly."

"And I'm thinking about it right now."

"I'd rather you think about how I look at you when we make love." With that, he burrowed inside, tunneling a few inches deep before retreating only far enough to press farther into her on the next pass.

Holly put her hand up, cupping the side of his face. She'd expected him to be experienced, to be skilled, but sweet? No, that hadn't been on her list of qualities Trent possessed.

Maybe she didn't know her husband as well as she'd thought.

A sigh floated from her parted lips when he lowered his head and began to kiss the side of her neck as he joined them together. In partnership. In this faux-marriage filled with very real sex. In an affair that would give them both what they needed to survive the next ninety days of their lives and set them up to not only endure, but to prosper, from then on.

"I'm not hurting you, am I?" he asked when she stiffened, thinking too much and forgetting to feel the incredible things he was doing to her with his hands, tongue, lips, and cock.

"Not at all." She widened her legs so he could fit more comfortably between them, sinking deeper into her in the process.

"Good. It's been a long time since I've done this." A flash of insecurity in his sky-blue gaze reengaged part of her brain.

"Had sex? Me too." She bit her lower lip, hoping that wouldn't make him slow down or, God forbid, stop. Because whatever he was doing felt way better than she'd expected. He was gliding into her, stroking nerve endings she hadn't even known she'd had with his thick erection, and moving in some sort of figure eight that ground his pelvis against her clit each time he bottomed out.

"Well, no. I meant have sex with a woman on my own."

"What is it you like so much about ménage? That's what your dad was so upset about, right?" If Holly's hands hadn't been full of Trent's muscles, she would have slapped herself on the forehead. "I mean, we can talk about that later. Sorry. Don't mean to distract you."

He laughed then kissed her, this time with more passion and less caution.

Perfect.

"I'm going to concentrate on making you scream in a second," he promised. "I can't say why I like it exactly. I've realized that's just how I am. Poly, like the rest of your friends. It feels right when I share. Lately, Lorenzo will bring a woman home from the club he works at and the three of us...you know."

"Ah. I mean, I can guess, but maybe you should tell me the details later." Holly couldn't concentrate on anything but how her body matched his so precisely.

"It doesn't freak you out?"

"Absolutely not. It makes me...curious. I want to hear all about it. Learn about you and what that kind of relationship is really like for you. Later, though."

"That sounds...great." He lowered himself to his elbows, planted on either side of her shoulders, and began to fuck more seriously, whiting out her mind and replacing any of her worries or stray thoughts with pure bliss.

It was as if her lack of censure motivated him to give her even more pleasure. If this was him out of his element, what would it be like to be sandwiched between him and his roommates?

She locked her legs around him, but that didn't prohibit him from plunging into her with a steady and unrelenting rhythm she couldn't resist for long. But she wanted him to fall with her, not be left hanging again.

"Trent..." She tried to explain.

"Go ahead." He grinned at her, then sped up. "Wring my cock with your tight pussy. Come all over me. I want to see it once at least before I let go too. But it's getting harder."

"It's already plenty hard."

He laughed, then smiled down at her. "I like you, Holly. I really do. Now shut up and come like I know you want to."

Fuck, he was right even if he had a smart mouth. So she let go and rode the wave of passion as he rode her, shuttling in and out throughout even the most intense of her spasms. Holly couldn't believe she'd thought that oral would be better than this, but then again, she'd never had sex with him before.

And she knew now, for sure, that the woman in the bushes that night hadn't been faking it.

Neither was she.

Her pussy had barely stopped spasming when he reached between them to rub her clit.

"You're gorgeous, Holly. So in tune with me. So perfect." He nipped her lower lip, keeping her riveted to his instruction. "This time, when you go over, I'm coming with you. I'm going to fill you. You're going to make me shoot so hard. You know that, right? It's for you, Holly. Because of you."

And just as he began to stutter in his lunges, losing control, a noise from the other room caught her attention.

"Where's the happy couple?" Lorenzo shouted as he stumbled through the front door, clearly having had a few more to drink since they'd last seen him.

Then he grunted, as if Owen had smacked him in the back of the head. "Shut up. Couldn't you hear them going at it while I was unlocking the door?"

"They're what?" Lorenzo cursed in Portuguese, but it didn't sound any farther away.

Trent looked over his shoulder, then back at her, but instead of stopping, his hips slapped against her pelvis, grinding, thrusting his cock as deep as it could go within her.

They hadn't bothered to shut the door all the way, having gotten completely distracted before they could. And in the gap, Holly could see his roommates glancing in their direction. Her pussy clenched, smothering Trent's cock.

It was like that night, except she was the woman in the rhododendrons. Enjoying the hell out of his hard body moving over her and within her and not giving a damn who knew it. Proud that he'd chosen her and that she was making him love it.

"You like that?" he groaned against her neck before raking his teeth over it. "That they know? That they can see me fucking you?"

His next thrust was a little more erratic, a little harder, too. She cried out.

Trent pressed himself onto his forearms so he could look into her eyes as he demanded, "Tell me."

"Yes," she hissed, shocked that it was true. But something about them knowing, witnessing it, made her feel sultry instead of slutty. As if a firework full of knowledge exploded over her, enlightening her, she understood why Kari and Andi swore by ménage even if she'd only had the slightest taste of what it could be like.

That's all it took, and she was flying.

Holly screamed Trent's name. She clutched his shoulders, trying and failing not to rake her nails over them. He grunted and burst into a flurry of motion, plowing into her hard and fast as he joined her.

True to his word, he flooded her pussy with jet after jet of his release.

He came so hard the headboard banged against the wall with each clench of his body.

And afterward, he melted onto her, smothering her with the most welcome weight and heat, his cock still embedded fully within her as they floated somewhere special and euphoric together.

It was a long, long time before she opened her eyes, but when she did the doorway was empty and dark. And if she thought she heard a long, low groan from the room next door, it was probably her imagination. Right?

Too afraid to ruin the best night of her life, Holly

didn't ask any questions. Instead, she drifted, half asleep, as Trent cleaned them both up, tucked her under the covers, and curled protectively around her, keeping her close to his spectacular body.

The last thing she remembered hearing was him whispering into the dark, "Sleep well, wifey."

10

———

Holly woke up to something wet on her cheek followed by adorable snuffles, a warm fuzzy body curling up next to her in bed, and...a tail whapping against her leg.

"What the...?" She blinked and reached around the rumpled sheets, finding no other person beside her.

Had she dreamed all that crazy shit about Trent?

The pleasant ache in her body and the crushing weight that had been lifted off her mind said otherwise. If not, then where had he wandered off to and what was a dog doing in bed with her instead? She sat up, pushing her hair off her face, and blinked several times to bring the room into focus.

She couldn't look down on Trent for existing essentially the same way they had in college—with basic, put-together furniture and roommates to divvy expenses —since she herself had reverted to living with her mom instead of venturing out on her own.

Deeply offended at being ignored, the brindle-coated

mutt whimpered, then head-butted her, making her chuckle before ruffling his floppy ears.

"Hey there, big guy. Why are you so cute?" She petted him as he blinked up at her with oddly familiar eyes and she wondered...

No, it couldn't be.

"I can't help it," Trent said with a smirk as he entered the room carrying a tray heaped with breakfast treats.

"I meant the dog." She grinned, as eager to see her husband as she was to devour the fluffy pancakes, bacon, and bowls of fruit he set down beside them.

"Ah, too bad." He nudged the pup from the bed so they could eat without his sad eyes begging for scraps he probably shouldn't have anyway. Proving Trent wasn't immune to the pitiful stare, he tossed the dog a slice of banana, which he inhaled without chewing.

"What's his name?"

"I decided to call him Moose. As a puppy, his paws were so huge they might as well have been hooves." Trent avoided meeting her gaze when he said, "I hope you aren't pissed that I didn't follow through on my promise."

"Which one?" She tensed, afraid he'd decided not to wire the cash Westford, Armand, and King had fronted them, based on the amount locked up in the trust, to her savings account after all. She wouldn't blame him or hold him to the contract Kari's guys and Cooper had drawn up for them the night before if he'd had a change of heart...or wallet.

Regardless, he'd given her one of the best nights of her life, even under unusual and distressing circumstances for them both. For that alone, she was grateful they'd reunited.

"My promise to take him to the shelter." Trent tipped his head, almost like the dog did as he watched his owner pop a slice of bacon between his lips. "I guess I just never got around to it."

"It *is* the same dog then?" Her heart expanded a little knowing that he hadn't been able to give the little guy up. She would have kept him herself if she'd been allowed.

"Yup." Trent shrugged. "I needed a friend at that point in my life, so I figured I'd give it a try."

"How the hell did he get so big?"

"He eats a ton." As if on cue, Moose plopped one of his ginormous paws on her thigh. She snuck him a bite of eggs. After all, Trent had easily cooked enough for the three of them to share.

"Where was he last night?" Holly had been pretty focused on Trent and what they did in bed, but she was sure she would have noticed if Moose had been there at the door to greet them.

"Our neighbor watches him when Lorenzo, Owen, and I work nights." Trent forked some eggs into his mouth as she plucked a few strips of bacon from the tray. "Although I guess I won't be doing that anymore unless there's stuff I have to do to set up the new business I can't finish during the day."

"That's a good thing, right?" She angled toward him to study his expression. He seemed utterly relaxed and even more handsome than she remembered. Maybe settling down, and getting laid, worked wonders for him.

"Yeah, definitely." He took a sip from his steaming mug of coffee before passing it to her to share. Somehow it seemed unbearably intimate even given what they'd done the night before...on their wedding night.

Holly choked as the repercussions of the past twenty-four hours began to sink in. This wasn't some extended date or even a pleasant morning after a one-night stand. This was her new reality.

And she was kind of okay with that. Maybe a little *too* okay with it.

"Are you freaking out yet?" Trent rescued the mug from her, then slammed coffee like he had his beer the night before, as if he needed the shot of caffeine to make it through this conversation, or maybe the next several months of their arrangement.

"Only a little." She took a deep, if shaky breath, then nibbled the corner off a slice of cinnamon toast.

"Good, because I keep waiting for the panic to kick in and I'm over here thinking I'm a weirdo because it isn't happening." Trent put his hand on her knee and squeezed. "Thank you, for being there for me last night and turning a horrible event into something wonderful."

"Don't make me sound like a martyr. You're returning the favor." She put her hand on his and rubbed her finger over his ring, which matched hers. "But I'm glad I could be there when you needed me."

"Same goes." He leaned in and stole a quick kiss. It might have become something more than that if they wouldn't have flung food all over his bed and tempted Moose beyond his training.

"So, uh, what's your last name?"

"*Your* last name is Bellini, if you want it to be." He smiled at her.

"I like peach bellinis." She laughed.

"I noticed last night." He grinned back. No matter what else happened, they'd had one hell of a time. Good, terrible, then excellent...in that order.

They ate in relative silence, having worked up quite an appetite together. She ate an extra pancake, saving some fuel for what she hoped would be a rematch later. But when she'd finished, she couldn't stop wondering how her mother was doing without her.

Sure, there was a nurse standing guard, and probably their neighbor too, but they didn't know where everything was or the way Holly did stuff. What if they needed help or couldn't find something important, like her mother's medicine?

"Do you mind if I call my mom quick? I need to check on her. I want to tell her the news and get the ball rolling on notifying her doctors, too."

"Of course not." He squeezed her hand. "I'll be so happy if something positive comes out of this whole fiasco."

She sort of thought something already had, but she best not forget that this was only a temporary arrangement. After ninety days, she'd be on her own again.

For now...she was going to make the most of it.

Trent must have been thinking along the same lines as her, which seemed to happen pretty often. "Why don't we go over there and do it together, in person?" he asked.

She chewed her final bits of food too slowly without responding.

"I mean, unless you're embarrassed of me or ashamed of what we're doing. I'm not trying to crowd you..."

"I don't think that's a good idea." She winced. "It's been tough just getting by for now. Our place isn't really made for visitors. It's basic and not the sort of place I'm proud of."

"Holly. I grew up in enormous estates, kept pristine by

a sizable staff. We had pretty much every convenience you could hope for, and look where it got me." He cleared his throat. "My own father despised and disowned me. My mother hasn't even responded to my texts since he passed away. Even now she's doing what he says. Hell, his will probably spells out that they're all to stay away from me lest they be corrupted by my evil ways."

Holly hugged him and rested her forehead on his neck, giving him the courage to keep going.

"What you and your mom have is way more valuable than anything money could buy. Except maybe a kidney, and we've got that covered, right?"

"Right. But..." Holly hesitated. She wished she could let him in, but it was too soon for that. Sex was one thing, the rest... No, not yet. And maybe not ever. "I just don't think we should do it in person. I don't want to overwhelm her or barge in without her being ready for more company."

"Okay. I understand." Trent put some space between them. He gathered up the dishes onto the tray and headed for the kitchen, Moose right on his heels. "I'll give you some privacy to talk to her. I have a feeling she might not be as thrilled as we are about the scheme all of us cooked up. Especially not about having a professional gambler for a son-in-law. Maybe you shouldn't tell her that part."

"It's nothing to do with you personally, Trent. I swear." Holly hated that her own insecurities had stung him with yet another rejection.

"It's okay." He smiled sadly at her. "I'm using her daughter. I wouldn't like me either if I were her. Go ahead, Holly. Call her. I'm going to clean up the kitchen and then take a shower."

Damn, was he a dream guy or what? Holly made a

pact then and there to show him how amazing she thought he was before their time was over.

But first...

She snagged her cell phone off the nightstand and dialed her mom. "Hey, Mom! Yes, last night was incredible. You're never going to guess what happened..."

Trent hovered over his laptop, reading and rereading his patent application for the thousandth time. He was going to take Cooper, Ford, Brady, and Josh up on their offer to review it before he submitted it, but he hadn't even gotten to the legalese yet and something felt...off.

"You okay?" When Holly put her hand on his shoulder and rubbed, he jumped. He hadn't heard her rouse or cross to his desk. Damn, he must have been really fucked up to be that out of it. Normally he noticed every tiny thing she did.

"Yeah, just getting the patent stuff ready. But this schematic..."

She came around and leaned her hip on his leg until he scooted his chair back and gathered her onto his lap. "You don't mind if I look at this, do you? I swear I'm not going to sell your trade secrets to the highest bidder."

"You're my wife. I think it's okay." He liked saying that more than he should.

Holly grinned like she always did when he teased

about it, then kissed him softly. He might have gotten distracted, or said fuck it to the application, if she hadn't stopped with hardly more than a peck and returned her attention to his screen.

She reached over and took the mouse, zooming in on the schematics so she could inspect every nut and bolt along with the wiring diagrams. Her eyes narrowed and she didn't ask a single question about the terms or parts he'd described in detail to the person he'd hired to design the schematics with his first six months of gambling winnings.

"Hang on..." He had a light bulb moment. "What was your major in school again?"

"Mechanical engineering." She grinned. "I haven't had a chance to actually use my degree yet, but if you don't mind, I think I could tweak this a bit and make a few improvements."

"Are you fucking kidding me?"

She went stiff on top of him and started to stand.

"I meant that in the best possible way, Holly." He looped his arms around her waist, refusing to let her go. "Of course you can help. I can't believe I got this lucky. A sexy wife who's the perfect partner in bed and out... Um, yes, please."

"You think I'm good in bed?" She pretended to focus on his drawings, but he could tell she was more interested in his opinion than she cared to let on.

"I've never come so hard in my life as I have the past few times we've been together." And that was no lie. It kind of blew his mind that he'd enjoyed sex with her as much as he had considering Lorenzo and Owen hadn't gotten involved. Of course, he wondered how much better he could make it for her if they went down that path.

He shifted her so she would be less likely to feel him getting hard thinking about it.

"Because of us...together...or because I let Lorenzo and Owen sneak a peek of us having sex?" Her voice got wispy, as if she was remembering, like he was. Or maybe because she was still shy about what she'd obviously gotten off on. Just like he had even though it was only a taste of what he usually preferred.

"Both," he answered honestly. "And if you ever want them to do more than watch, or if you want to see what's up between you without me, that's fine too. You're free to do whatever you want as far as I'm concerned."

"Right. Because we're not really married." Holly cursed under her breath. "It would be best if neither of us forgot that this little experiment will be over soon."

As usual, she was right. And he wasn't about to make things worse by talking about it more.

"Okay. But until then...will you help me?" he wondered.

Holly nodded. She highlighted the area that had been bugging him. "You need to adjust the wiring harness here to avoid long-term chafe that will shorten the life of each panel and cause you warranty issues. You can do that by changing this cross member to a piece of U-shaped aluminum and adding a conduit to run the wire through that protected area."

"Damn it!" Yes, that's exactly what he hadn't been able to figure out. She'd taken one glance and spotted it immediately. "You're right. That's especially important because my goal is to make these so low cost to produce that for every solar panel we sell domestically, we can donate one to a developing nation. It would be my dream to really make a difference instead of pumping up my bank account like my father did his whole life. There has to be something more than that, right?"

Holly relaxed against him. She pivoted, hugging him tight as she smiled warmly up at him. "Yeah, that's an amazing goal. I want to help. Have you built a prototype yet?"

"Sort of, but I bet you can make it better." He wasn't sure why it made him sheepish to admit his nerdy habits, maybe because he knew she was into the frat boy she thought of him as. "Tinkering with electronics is my hobby, but I was dumb and didn't take many classes that are actually helpful with that side of things. My father insisted I be a business major and if I'd argued, he would have refused to pay my tuition."

"At least you'll know how to bring this to market." Holly perked up. "Didn't Owen mention something about a corresponding battery technology to store the power you generate?"

"Yeah, that's phase two of the project. I'm still tinkering with getting that as ready for production as the panels are. I have a workshop out in the garage. Want to see?"

"Hell, yes." She bolted off his lap so fast he'd have been disappointed if it wasn't for the opportunity to geek out on his hobby with her. Lorenzo and Owen patiently listened to him ramble about his inventions, but they didn't have any real interest or understanding in the shit he spent every hour he wasn't gambling or sleeping on.

Holly did. *Damn.*

Trent grinned as he took her hand and led her to his laboratory as eagerly as he'd guided her to bed the night before. Moose trotted along behind them. And with that, they were off down the rabbit hole of his creations and how, together, they could make the world a better place for a lot of people while also making a shit ton of money.

Win. Win. Win. And win some more, especially if Holly ever decided to take him up on his offer to explore with Owen and Lorenzo.

12

—————

Trent looked up from working on the new battery module that would be the ideal companion to the solar panels he and Holly had damn near perfected, and realized time was flying by. Days filled with finally progressing on his project were only surpassed by nights in bed with her. He could get used to this. Hell, he already had.

"Hey, Hol, guess what?"

"Hmm?" She nudged her adorably thick black reading glasses up her nose and blinked at him, as entrenched in their tinkering as he had been a moment ago.

"It's our one-week anniversary." Trent smiled at her.

She didn't mirror his expression. Instead, she frowned. "Time is going so fast. The three months will be up before you know it."

Rather than brood on that fact, which had the power to ruin his good mood, Trent asked, "How hungry are you?"

"Getting there." She rubbed her softly rounded stomach, reminding him of how amazing it felt to lie on top of her while he surrounded himself with her heat and slickness.

And now he was craving more than dinner.

"I can order a meal for us. Something fancy, if you want to celebrate." It felt odd to have extra cash to spend on stuff like that after he'd been so damn careful for so long, hoarding every penny to reach his aspirations. "Or..."

"What's behind door number two?" she asked with a cute grin that made him want to impress her.

"If you can wait a little longer, I'll order ingredients from the market and cook for you myself."

"You know how?" She grinned. "Let's do that. I can help if you show me what to do."

That sounded...domestic, almost fucking ordinary. Like something a boyfriend and girlfriend would do on a date. Sure, she was his wife, but he wasn't kidding himself. It was in name only, so he should take the chance to play house with her while he could.

"You seemed to like the scallops at Kari's party." How the fuck had that only been a week ago? "Want me to order seafood? I make a mean rainbow trout meunière."

"I have no idea what that is, but I trust you." She nodded, then turned back to the part she'd been fine-tuning.

Could she really have that much faith in him after so short a time? They had spent every minute of it together and hadn't argued once. It seemed almost too easy. If life had taught him anything, it was that they hadn't run into the hard stuff yet.

That didn't keep him from wishing things could stay like they were forever.

Shaking himself from his thoughts, he opened his

shopping app and added the ingredients he'd need to his cart. On a whim, he tossed in a few candles and a nice bottle of wine to go with it. Spouse or not, Holly was his lover and his business partner. He wanted to make the night special for them both.

The next hour raced by as they tweaked another component he had already thought was as good as it could get, until she showed him differently.

Only Moose going nuts like he always did when someone rang the doorbell broke Trent from his focus.

"Ah shit, the groceries." He jogged into the house and collected a bunch of bags from the delivery guy before kicking the door closed. When he turned, Holly was there, offering to take some and help him unpack. He let her, impressed again by how seamlessly they worked together.

It wasn't long before she'd set the low table in the living room, lit the candles, and poured them each a glass of wine while he breaded the thin fillets and began poaching the green beans he'd gotten to go along with them. For a while she watched him as he lost himself in the motions, sort of like he did when they were building things in the workshop.

"Where'd you learn how to do this?" Holly wondered from where she leaned against the island watching him squeeze a lemon over the sizzling fillets when they were just about finished, golden brown.

"My parents had a staff including several chefs. I used to hang out in the kitchen with them when I could escape my nannies to see how they made stuff." He shrugged. "Except once I saw how they lived and worked for what we took for granted, or a lot less to be honest, it started to feel wrong to enjoy their meals without pitching in."

Holly brought two plates over and held them out for

him to load up. "I think that's really sweet."

"It used to piss my dad off so bad. Especially because he caught me helping them out after it became apparent to us both that I didn't give two shits about learning how to run his empire or shout at employees in business meetings." Trent shook his head. "We really couldn't have been more different. I used to wish I could have been the person he wanted me to be. But then I realized I'd hate myself too."

"You didn't hate him. And that's why it hurts so much." Holly carried their dinners into the other room and set them on the low table.

He was prepared to shoo Moose away before he stole her meal, but instead the dog behaved himself, curling up right beside her without even begging Trent for a morsel. Either he was sick, or he was as devoted to Holly as Trent was starting to think he could become.

They were as comfortable sharing quiet moments as they were during the exciting discoveries they made at work or while having sex. For a while, they ate, simply enjoying his handiwork.

After forking the last bite into her mouth, Holly moaned. "That was incredible. Thank you."

"Any time." Trent studied her profile in the warm, flickering glow of the candle, then followed her arm downward to where she was petting Moose. He'd never been so jealous of the mutt before.

And suddenly he knew that their evening wasn't going to end with dessert.

Because he was still hungry. For her.

Trent reached out and took her chin in his hand, angling her face toward him so he could look into her eyes. Relaxed and satisfied, she was even more alluring than she'd been shaking her fine ass in that flashy dress the night he'd sworn he had to finally have her.

Holly was peaceful, steady, and someone he could get used to relying on. To partnering with. In all aspects of his life. Especially in bed.

Or on the couch, for that matter.

He leaned in and so did she. They met in the middle, lips on lips. He wasn't sure how long they made out, but at some point he realized she'd straddled him and was sitting in his lap, his hands cupping her ass and using his grip to pull her tight to him.

His cock rubbed against her softness through his sweats. It wasn't close enough to her.

Without thinking, he took the oversized T-shirt she'd borrowed from him and drew it over her head, watching her auburn hair tumble down around her shoulders and her perky breasts. And that's when it hit him that they were getting naked, right there in the living room.

"We should take this to my bedroom." He glanced over at the clock. "It's getting late. Lorenzo and Owen could be home soon."

It shocked the hell out of him when she didn't immediately agree. Instead, she murmured, "Would you hate it if they saw us fucking? Like the first time, except...more."

If his cock hadn't already been mostly hard, that would have done it on its own.

He rocked his hips upward, pressing his erection against her core so she could tell exactly what he thought of the naughty possibility.

"Is that a hypothetical question, or would you like to do an official experiment and see for yourself?" He sure as hell wasn't going to argue if she wanted to test the waters.

Lorenzo and Owen had both made it clear they were available for any and all sexcapades. Not only because that's how they usually rolled, but they were twice as interested because of Holly. And Trent didn't blame them. She was beautiful, smart, loyal, and kind. Selfless.

So what if she was only doing this for his benefit?

He didn't like that thought. So he rose, intending to walk her backward until they fell on his bed together.

"No, Trent." She pulled at his clothes, dragging his pants down to his ankles. "I can't wait anymore. I've been dying all day. Fuck me here. Now. Please. And if they come home...maybe it was meant to be."

He growled as he kicked off his pants and socks, then tossed his shirt after them.

When he lunged for her, she was naked too.

They tumbled onto the couch together, her conveniently beneath him as he stared into her eyes. "For the record, if you're ever horny during the day, you should say so. I'd love to fuck you on my workbench."

"Someday. Soon. But not now." She was already spreading her legs, inviting him inside. It had only been ten or twelve hours since they'd last been fused, but he already had the longing to join with her so intimately she couldn't simply walk away from what they shared at the end of their contract.

This couldn't possibly be how all her relationships were, could it?

Because he'd never craved anyone like he did her.

Trent bit her neck as he took his hard-on in his fist and guided it to her. She gasped and tossed her head back as he entered her, trying to give her time to adjust despite her sharp little claws digging into his shoulders, urging him to advance.

He'd barely managed to work himself fully within her silky grasp when, sure enough, a key slid into the door. He froze but she didn't, rocking her hips upward to fuck herself on him when he stayed still. "You're sure?"

She moaned, then shuddered beneath him as if the thought alone was going to make her come around him. Holy shit.

Trent couldn't wait any longer. He began to pump into her, both of them groaning in unison as his cock tunneled through her tight muscles. And when he heard Lorenzo curse behind them and start to leave, he looked over his shoulder without breaking stride. "Welcome home."

Lorenzo looked at him, then at Owen behind him, then at Holly, who was chuckling even as her eyes rolled back. He wasn't stupid. The man came inside and strode to the armchair nearby. Owen plopped into the matching one on the other side so both of them had an unobstructed front-row seat to their show.

Trent thought he might shoot then and ruin everything. Although he knew that if he came too soon, either of his friends would be more than willing to take care of Holly until he'd recovered enough to finish things properly. But was she ready for that?

Or did having them watch do enough for her?

Holly bit her lip and looked up at him. "I'm so close. Fuck me, Trent. Don't stop now."

"I wasn't planning on it." It wasn't enough, what they were doing, sliding along each other like two teenagers who'd been left unsupervised a few minutes too many. Trent had to fuck her hard, deeper, and show his roommates that she was the one. For him and maybe for them too.

He withdrew, the strangled moan she made at the loss of his cock giving him a big head. Both sorts.

Transferring his weight to the foot planted on the floor, he stood, then held out his hand to her.

"I told you, I don't want to go to your room." She pouted as she refused to take it.

Trent laughed, a deep rumble he hardly recognized from himself. "Good. That's not the plan. Now come over here so I can finish what I started."

"Oh." Holly looked even more adorable with her cheeks stained red. "Okay."

She didn't fight him when he half-lifted her, keeping her steady until he could lead her around to the end of the sofa. He hugged her from behind, her back pressed to his chest and abs, her breasts filling his palms. She tucked into the curve of his torso, exactly the right fit.

So when he leaned forward, she had no choice but to bend too, putting her ass and pussy on display for his best friends.

"Shit, yes." Lorenzo hissed in Portuguese with a few more curses that Trent didn't have the brainpower to interpret right then. He tossed a wicked grin at his friend, noticing that Lorenzo was rubbing himself over his jeans, waiting for Trent to bury himself in Holly once more.

It was as if he was imagining it was him fucking her, or maybe both of them doing it together.

Maybe one night soon it would be that way. But for right then his friends were going to have to live vicariously through him as they gradually introduced Holly to their desires. If they scared her away, if she condemned them like his father had, he wasn't sure he could take that.

His cock lost some of its steel.

"Oh no. Fuck that." Owen glared at him. "You're not going to ruin this for us. Get in there."

Holly glanced over her shoulder, rousing from the sexual haze she'd fallen into as their bodies fed off each other's energy. No, he couldn't have that.

So he clasped his cock in his hand and pumped it a few times.

"I don't want to be the only one naked. Tell them to show me how much they like watching us. Can I see them like this?" Holly asked.

Owen had already jammed one hand beneath his shirt. When Trent flicked his gaze to the other man and nodded, his friend undid his pants. His cock sprang free, landing on his abdomen. He licked his palm, then stroked it as Lorenzo hurried to catch up.

Holly studied each of them and how they touched themselves while he matched their sharp jerks on his own cock.

It only took a few passes before he drove anything but the thought of sinking back into Holly's sweet pussy from his mind. Perfect. Just like every time they shared a woman, he was nearly overwhelmed with pleasure. And this time it was a whole new level.

Because he gave a shit about Holly. And wanted her to experience more than just a solid orgasm or two. He wanted this to mean something to her too.

Trent didn't want her to forget him or this night once their sham was over.

Sometime when he wasn't about to fuck her senseless, he'd have to think about why that might be. Sometime a lot later.

Trent cupped her perfect ass, his thumb spreading her apart so that the slickness of her pussy was impossible to miss. He reached between her legs to cup her mound and rubbed the palm of his hand over her clit. She moaned and ground on it, making him sure that she wasn't going to last any longer than he was.

He couldn't wait to feel her hugging his cock as she lost control.

So he advanced, removing his hand and placing it on the dip of her waist to hold her steady. His cock hung heavy, the tip nudging her core. The instant they made contact again, she groaned and tried to wriggle backward.

That did nothing to aid his self-control.

Trent used two fingers to aim his erection as he impaled her, going balls-deep in a single unbearably long stroke. Her ass cushioned him, slowing his momentum as he bottomed out in her. The arm of the couch seemed to work its magic on her clit.

She went up onto her tiptoes and braced her hands on the couch cushions, practically begging him to do it again, harder and faster than before. So he did.

Trent fucked her like he hadn't had sex in ten years. He leaned forward, putting his hand lightly around her neck to keep her in place. She screamed and practically squeezed him from her body.

Lorenzo and Owen were watching like he and Holly made the best porn on earth. Their hands flew over their cocks. This wasn't going to be one of their legendary marathon sessions. The tension was too intense already for that.

No, it wasn't going to take much to set them all off.

Owen could see that he was struggling, so he helped out. "Holly, you're so gorgeous. I love watching him fuck you like this. You were made for his dick."

She clawed at the couch, her body rippling around

Trent as it gathered for her climax.

When Lorenzo saw how Owen's reassurance affected her, he piled on. "I've wanted to see this every night since that first one, when we caught a peek. Having to listen to the two of you get it on and only being able to imagine how incredible this looks has been torture. Thank you for letting us watch you come apart like this. Let us watch you fly."

"Do it, Holly. Come for Trent," Owen cheered her on. "It's going to feel so good when you shatter around his big fat cock."

"Yes!" she screamed, and did as they instructed. She called his name and then exploded. Her pussy undulated, nearly forcing him from her body as he sank deep and let go. His release matched hers. Maybe even exceeded it, both of them writhing against each other as they were drained.

And when he pulled out, causing his seed to spill from her body, Lorenzo couldn't resist a moment longer. He arched, his muscles standing out as they seemed ready to rip from his bones. His neck was a stony column as he groaned and his hips jerked.

Come flew from the tip of his cock, then spilled down his knuckles as he shouted a curse or maybe his thanks.

"Wow," Holly whispered, still panting as Trent gathered her into his arms and cradled her on his lap on the couch.

Before Lorenzo had finished putting on his show for her, Owen joined him. He roared, leaning back on the chair. He painted himself with come, showing her just how much she'd impacted him with her acceptance and her innate sensuality.

Holly shivered. Their pleasure drew out more of her

own. She was made for this. For them. If only he could figure out how to keep her.

Trent locked his arms around her. He wished it could be that easy.

The guys grabbed some extra napkins off the table and began to clean themselves up before tucking themselves away as if nothing out of the ordinary had just occurred when their lives had been altered forever.

"Soooo...that was fun." Holly giggled. "Thanks."

Trent's heart melted where she laid her head to hide her telltale blush against his pecs.

As if they could sense his unusual selfishness or the need to take things cautiously, Owen and Lorenzo hesitated before crossing the gap between their chairs and the couch. Over Holly's head, Trent shook his head no once.

They'd pushed her far enough for this first introduction to their wicked ways.

Maybe next time the guys could touch her, once she'd had a chance to process everything they'd done and decide if she wanted more without the influence of pheromones or serotonin flooding her brain.

After they'd had a chance to talk about what had happened and how she'd like to move forward. He hated the tiny sliver of himself that was worried if they fucked up this stuff, the very personal parts of their relationship, that he might lose out on either his business partner or his key to his father's checkbook.

Disgusted with himself, he unintentionally tightened his grip on her, making her squirm away. "Ow."

He hadn't meant to hurt her. But his possessiveness, something he'd never experienced before, had the power to do that, and he had better remember it, too.

"Sorry." He kissed her temple and relaxed his grip, settling into the cushions but keeping her as close as ever when he did. "You ready for bed?"

She laughed softly. "Yeah, but only if you actually mean for sleeping. I don't think I could go another round if I tried. Not even if you say so this time."

Trent chuckled too. "No worries. I'm all out of steam myself. That was...epic."

"It was." She kissed his jaw, then stared at Owen and Lorenzo dreamily.

"Come on, Moose." He stood, lifting Holly, who instinctively wrapped her legs around him and rested her head on his shoulder, hugging him loosely as he made his way to his room.

When he got there, he laid her on the bed, then crawled in after her, using the voice command of the home automation system to turn the lights off, more thankful than he'd ever been in his life that he didn't have to get up again or spend a moment away from her.

Instead, he rolled to his side and spooned her, circling one arm around her waist. He kissed her cheek, not entirely surprised to see her lashes lying heavy on her cheeks.

They'd have to talk about what they'd done, and what he'd like to do in the future, some other time. Tomorrow. Neither of them was capable of logic or consciousness right then.

And even if they had been, he'd be too scared of wrecking the mood and the rare satisfaction that coursed through him as he cradled Holly all night long with Moose curled up at their feet and his best friends not far away.

13

"Thanks for trusting me enough to meet your mom, finally." Trent put his hand in his coat pocket, the other holding on to Moose's leash. They walked at a brisk pace past tidy rock-garden lawns and palm tree landscapes even though she wished they were running in the other direction, back to his house and the bubble they'd been living in together.

"I didn't exactly have a choice." Holly tried not to pout.

"What does that mean?" His gorgeous blue eyes narrowed.

"Um, well, my mom insisted on meeting you. She said it's to say thank you for everything you've done for her, but don't be fooled." She focused on their feet, which walked in sync without even trying. "She's nosy. It's been two weeks and she wouldn't put up with my excuses a moment longer."

"She wants to see what kind of creeper you're shacking up with?" Trent's frown only reinforced her belief that this was a horrible idea. He was already sensitive after the damage his family had wrought on his self-esteem and his ego. He didn't need her mom giving him the third degree because she couldn't believe someone would be as generous as Trent without serious strings.

"Pretty much. The fact that Andi, Kari, and their guys vouched for you is probably the only reason she hasn't already called the police to come and rescue me from you." Holly groaned.

Her mother was convinced that Trent secretly wanted her and was using the cash as some kind of leverage to hook up with her until he got bored. Holly couldn't even deny they were sleeping together, because every moment they weren't working on his plans or the business or securing some kind of pre-authorizations from the insurance company, they were getting it on. They both needed to decompress and endless orgasms worked pretty damn well for that.

Her mother knew her well enough to bust any attempt at a lie

"Let's just say she doesn't approve of me marrying—or whatever else—for a kidney."

"Then we'll have to show her that we're a great team regardless of how we got matched up." Trent took his hand out of his pocket and clasped hers in it. It was warm from his coat and felt so reassuring and familiar even after a few short weeks.

Holly's stomach knotted. For a hot second she'd thought he was going to say *then we'll have to show her that we're an actual couple* or *then we'll have to show her that we're falling for each other despite our dumb contract.*

She should have known better.

Maybe her mother was right. After tonight and assessing things for herself, she wouldn't hesitate to tell Holly if she was making a giant mistake, like looking at things through rose-colored glasses or being willfully ignorant so that she could pretend—even for three months—that she'd found someone she could try to build a future with.

The rest of the walk was quiet as they both prepared for the inquisition ahead. When they entered her neighborhood, ten minutes or so later, Holly found every step harder to take than the last. By the time she was crossing the cracked sidewalk, her feet felt like they had been cast from lead.

"Is it really so awful to introduce me to your mom?" Trent frowned. "I know I'm not exactly boyfriend material, but..."

"Hey." She turned toward him, patting Moose, who nearly plowed into her as she stopped abruptly. He was antsy, picking up on their tension. "That's not it at all."

In fact, it was exactly the opposite. She wished they'd bumped into each other at the convenience store on the corner months ago and made up for the time they'd lost at college and afterward, and that she was really bringing him home to show off her perfectly average lover.

Instead, she was thinking about how to conceal the feelings she could no longer deny she was starting to have for him from the one person who knew her best in the world. Because if her mom realized Holly had a crush on her own husband, her mom might not be as willing to let her continue her ruse and risk getting hurt at the end of it all.

It would be exactly like her to turn down a kidney to protect her daughter.

And that couldn't happen. All of the paperwork had been submitted, their bank account balance verified, doctors consulted, and her mother had been cleared for surgery. They were just waiting for the call...

Holly squeezed Trent's hand, then dragged him up the three stairs to the front door before knocking and letting herself in. She called around the partially open door, "Hey, Mom. I'm home."

Except it didn't feel like it.

Okay, so the tiny apartment really never had. But now that she'd started making herself comfy at Trent's place, it already felt more like where she belonged than this shithole ever had, despite the fact that her mother didn't seem to mind the "cozy" apartment half as much as she had.

To her it had more in common with a prison than a sanctuary, and every minute she'd spent there had been filled with anxiety and a sense of impending doom. Coming back brought all that negativity bubbling to the surface.

The home health aide had helped her mother to a chair at the table, where a big bowl of spaghetti sat next to a plate of bread and butter. Not extravagant by any means and certainly not to someone who'd grown up wealthy, but Holly knew what that much effort would have cost her mom, even with assistance.

"Shit," Trent hissed under his breath, too low for Holly's mom to hear as he trailed a step or two behind her.

Holly glanced over her shoulder, her brow raised.

"I should have brought flowers. I'm sorry," he spoke up as he shook his head. "I told you I suck at this."

From the table, Holly's mom laughed. "It's the thought that counts. That's very sweet of you. I'm just glad to have my daughter back for an evening, and to meet you too."

Before Trent could respond, Moose wormed away and

bounded into the kitchen, his tail whapping every piece of furniture he passed in the tight quarters. He bolted to Holly's mom and began licking her enthusiastically. Maybe because he could smell the food or maybe because he was as smart as he sometimes seemed.

He knew who the boss was and how to win her over.

Holly's mom laughed and ruffled his ears even as Trent, horrified, finished taking off his shoes. He abandoned them on the mat by the door before rushing to claim his pet. "Moose! Behave!"

"He's fine. So handsome. Yes, he is." Holly's mom settled Moose with a few more pats. He promptly curled up at her feet, his tongue lolling out of his mouth.

"I think so too," Holly joked, looking at Trent instead of the dog.

Mom extended her hand to Trent. "Sorry I can't meet you halfway."

He earned a ton of points in Holly's book when, instead of taking her hand to shake it, he leaned in and gave her mom a hug. "You're fine right there, Mrs. Hendricks. It's so nice to finally meet you. Holly talks about you constantly. I feel like I know you already."

"I'm so sorry you have to put up with that." Mom laughed until she coughed a bit.

Holly winced. Both because she hadn't realized that she spent so much of their time together ruminating over her mother's condition and the rough road that still remained ahead for her.

They sat down and for a while enjoyed the food and easy conversation in peace. It was great to watch her mom eat nearly half a plate of spaghetti since her appetite had been drastically lacking as depression over her condition had set in, exacerbating her symptoms. The doctors had told them she needed to be as strong as possible for her operation, and it looked like Mom was doing her part to be up to par.

Holly battled the odd resentment that flashed through her heart. Mom was doing absolutely fine without her around to hover and fuss.

Maybe Holly wasn't quite as needed as she'd thought.

That should be great news, but it was hard to imagine what she might be if she wasn't the caretaker she'd considered herself the past few years.

There were too many things racing through her head, making her wonder where her place was in the world and what she was doing with her life. What would she be if the people she thought needed her—her mom and now Trent—didn't have a use for her anymore?

Nothing.

No one.

As she watched the two people she was closest to aside from Kari and Andi enjoying a good meal together, she got more and more on edge. Which was probably why she didn't handle it well when the pleasantries were concluded and the conversation turned more serious.

"You know, I was really worried when Holly told me what she'd done." Her mom smiled ruefully at them both, as if they were a real couple who'd eloped instead of co-conspirators.

"I can understand that. But we both needed something and this was the best way to get it. I promise I'm not trying to take advantage of her or anything like that." Trent frowned, as if he was regretting that last scoop of spaghetti. Was it the food or the topic giving him heartburn?

"I can see that." Holly's mom grinned at him.

"Please don't think that makes me some kind of saint or something." Trent's denial seemed harsh compared to the rest of their discussion. Holly knew he was thinking of his roommates and what he enjoyed doing with them. Sharing with them. She crossed her legs. "I'm not. Hell, my own father couldn't even love me."

"People are flawed, Trent." Holly's mom patted his hand. "No one's perfect, and some less so than others. I'm sorry your dad didn't appreciate what he had in you. I'll never make that same mistake. I hope you know, daughter, how much you mean to me. That you would even consider doing this for me, although I was angry and scared at first, means the world. I love you."

Holly blinked back tears as she took Mom's other hand in hers. The three of them were linked, joined by her mother. "I love you too."

Trent stood up abruptly, making his chair scrape on the crappy linoleum. "You know, I think I should go."

"That's not necessary." Holly's mom turned toward him, but he was already rinsing his plate and putting it in the dishwasher.

"Mrs. Hendricks, it was a pleasure to meet you, but, as usual, your daughter was right. I don't want to spoil the time you have together, since I realize I've cut that short lately while we've been working on my project." He turned toward Holly. "You stay. I'm going to review the engineer's report that came back today. I'll see you later, unless you plan to spend the night here."

"I hadn't, no." Holly glanced away because it would hurt too much if she realized he was bored of her already. Completely spooked by her mom picking up on the hints of something that could be real between them. "But maybe I should."

"Whatever you think is best." Trent gave her a loose, one-armed hug, then kissed her cheek. "See you...soon, I guess. Goodnight, ladies. Come on, Moose. We're going home."

When the dog refused to budge from Holly's mom's side, Trent growled, in a tone she'd never heard from him before. "Now, Moose. We have to leave."

The dog got to his feet slowly and licked Mom's hand one last time before trotting to his owner's side, shooting a backward glance at Holly as if to ask why she wasn't coming too.

Before she could convince herself to go with them, Trent left, without even asking if she'd like to join him instead. Holly braced herself on the back of her chair, trying not to collapse after he'd yanked the rug out from under whatever was blossoming between them.

"Holly..."

"Yeah, Mom?" She really wasn't in the mood to be criticized or to hear *I told you so*. Especially not after Trent had unwittingly stomped on her heart.

"He's a good guy. You were smart to trust him and to do this. For me. And for us." Mom folded her napkin neatly and laid it on her plate. "Thank you, honey. Now go catch up to him and his adorable dog before he gets too far away. I don't want you walking all the way to his house alone in the dark and we both know you're not staying here. You need to be there to figure out whatever just went sideways between you."

"Don't worry, Mom." Holly sighed. "I won't do anything to put your kidney transplant at risk."

Her mother reached out, faster than Holly thought her capable of, and lightly swatted her butt as if she were still five.

"Holly Faith Hendricks, you know a damn kidney doesn't mean anything compared to you. That man could make you happy, for many, many years, long after I'm gone." Her mother glared at her. "So don't screw this up... not for my benefit, but for yours. Stop him. Tell him that you care for him, flaws and all, and not for his money."

"Mom, it hasn't been very long. I don't think that's a good idea."

"Of course it is!" Her mother starting to rise even though it made her wheeze.

"Okay, I'm going." Holly pressed her back, adjusting the pillow behind her like she liked it. "Calm down, please. I'll take care of this. Don't worry."

Her mother relaxed then and smiled. "Maybe he really is what I've been wishing for."

Great. Now her own mother was on Team Trent. How disappointed was she going to be on the ninety-first day of their arrangement? Probably only half as crushed as Holly herself.

14

Holly hated to admit it, but walking home—or rather, to Trent's house—in the dark, by herself, something she never would have thought twice about before, kind of unsettled her without him and Moose by her side.

Damn it, she was already getting used to having them, and his roommates, around.

Her mother's advice swirled through her head, but she needed to hash things out with people who could truly understand, and with whom she didn't cringe when discussing sex.

She pulled her phone from her pocket and opened her messaging app, clicking the videochat icon on her group conversation with Andi and Kari. It hadn't rung more than a second or two before they both connected.

"There you are!" Andi leaned forward, as if she was scrutinizing every detail of Holly's ragged expression on her screen. Great.

"It's been forever. I hope you were too busy in bed with

Trent—or maybe Trent and a few of his roommates—to remember your dear old friends." Kari laughed.

"Why aren't you laughing?" Andi wondered. "What's wrong?"

Holly blinked against the tears that immediately threatened. What the hell?

"Oh no." Andi tipped her head. "You two hate each other and ninety days together is going to be torture."

"Not exactly." Holly looked up at the twinkling stars for a moment before filling them in about how incredible the past two weeks had been, both in bed and out of it. How they were working together on his inventions and the business that would get them out to the world. And even about what had happened with Lorenzo and Owen...

"Did that skeeve you out? Is that the problem?" Kari wondered.

"Um, nope. Not that either." She hoped they couldn't see her blushing. "I kind of liked them watching."

Understatement of the century.

"Ahhh, I get it." Andi's glare turned into a great big smile. "You *like* him! Like really, really like him."

"*And* his roommates!" Kari bounced in her seat. "This is perfect!"

"Except that it's not." Holly gripped the phone tighter. "It's not going to last and I'm stupid to hope otherwise, even for a moment. He just stormed out of a dinner with my mom. I think things are moving too fast for him. I'm a convenient lay, that's all. And it was obviously a bad idea to bring him home like he's really my boyfriend or some shit. Especially because now my mom likes him too. I'm so screwed."

"First of all." Andi held up her index finger. "You're both adults, free to do as you please. If what you're doing feels good and you're both onboard, keep doing that, for however long you can. And second, until you've talked to him about what's really going on in his head, you shouldn't assume anything. He has a lot of baggage, Holly. I didn't realize quite how much until the night of Kari's party."

Kari nodded. "She's right. Find him. Talk to him. Be honest and see where it takes you. I know it's scary as hell, but it could be worth it if things work out between you. Sure, this started for money, but maybe it will end up for..."

"Don't say it." She couldn't even bear to think of rainbows and hearts when it felt like they'd taken a huge step backward. "But you're right. I'm going to hash things out with him. I'm almost there now."

"Text us when you make it safe so we don't send Trent, Lorenzo, and Owen out to search for you. I mean, unless you want them to hunt you down and get all growly and protective. That could be a fun game, too." Andi giggled.

Holly rolled her eyes. "Not everything is about sex."

"Not everything. But enough." Kari grinned. "Just think, you could be about to have amazing make-up sex. I bet Lorenzo and Owen would be more than willing to help him apologize right."

Holly put her hand over her face, feeling the heat of her skin on her palm, mostly because she hoped they were right. And that was probably something else they needed to discuss. They'd avoided the subject since she'd watched the men jerk off while Trent fucked her.

"Okay, I'm almost there. No one send the National Guard." Holly said her goodbyes and disconnected before anyone inside Trent's house could hear the thoughts her friends were putting in her mind.

It was only when she arrived on his doorstep that she realized she didn't even have a key.

Lamely, she knocked on the door of what she had come to think of as her own house. Hopefully her mom—plus Kari and Andi—was right and she wasn't digging herself deeper into a dead-end situation.

When the door opened, she tried not to be disappointed. It wasn't Trent. With an awkward wave, she said, "Hi, Lorenzo."

"Hey, Holly." He frowned. "Where's your key?"

"I, uh, don't have one." She wrung her hands, wondering if it was too late to bolt back to her mother's house and forget the obvious bullshit her friends had been pumping her up with.

He stepped aside and ushered her in out of the chilly evening. "Sorry about that. Here, let me get you one of our spares."

"You better not. Maybe Trent didn't give me one on purpose." She hesitated on the threshold, wondering if she'd worn out her welcome already.

"Nah. Trent has been so preoccupied, he's not thinking straight." Lorenzo took her hand in his and led her inside, closing the door after her so she couldn't bolt back into the night like a frightened jackrabbit. "Especially when it comes to you."

Before she could insist—partially because she was trying to figure out what exactly he meant by that—Lorenzo had crossed to the kitchen and opened the junk drawer. She followed him in, trying not to notice how fluid and graceful his movements always were, almost like he was floating. She leaned her hip against the island, then asked, "So where is he anyway? Hasn't he come home yet? There's no way I beat him here."

"He stopped in to change clothes quick, then took Moose for a run. Hardly said a word to me." Lorenzo placed the key in her hand and curled her fingers around it but didn't let go. "Is everything okay, *xuxu*? He usually only does that when he's aggravated and needs to blow off steam."

Holly winced. "I think I mashed his buttons."

Lorenzo's warmth surrounding her fingers was comforting, especially when he brushed his thumb over her knuckles. She leaned in and tried not to notice how damn good he smelled, like spice and leather. It was his insight she was after, not his admittedly fine body.

"That's easy to do." Lorenzo smirked as he guided her toward the couch and sat down beside her.

She tried not to think about what had happened the last time they'd shared the living room together, but it was no use. Especially not when he put his arm around her shoulder and encouraged her to lay her head on his shoulder as he soothed her with his gentle words and his utter calm.

She couldn't imagine seeing him get angry. He just wasn't that sort of man.

And right now she needed that steady, sure comfort he provided so naturally.

He rubbed her arm from her elbow to her shoulder as he explained, "Look, Trent is my best friend. He's a great guy. But he's also fucked up, if you hadn't noticed."

"Who of us isn't?" She leaned into him, grateful for the sounding board.

"I am for sure." Lorenzo surprised her by admitting it so easily.

"What's your deal?" She made the mistake of looking

up at him then, his stare faraway as his angular jaw clenched.

"Nothing as dramatic as Trent's family disowning him or anything." He shrugged, making her head rise and fall where it rested on his muscular shoulder. "I got left at the altar in front of all my friends and family back in Brazil. After that, I decided a traditional relationship wasn't worth the trouble. Mostly, I stick to flirting with women at work. It's fine to take their dollar bills, too. Sometimes it goes as far as making their night extra special, bringing them home to play with me, Trent, and Owen before taking them back to whatever group of friends they're visiting Vegas with after we bring their fantasies to life. They get what they want and I have a bit of what I need, for a few hours anyway."

Holly angled toward him more, resting her palm on his rock-hard abs when she looked up at him. "Call it what you want, but I hear what you're not saying. Your ex broke your heart, and now you're afraid to open up or date someone on your own. But you like the attention of all these women because it reassures you that you're desirable."

"I guess you could see it that way." Lorenzo let his head drop back against the cushion. "Hell, maybe that is how it started even. But now...I like the way we do things. Together. We each have our strengths and it's a rush to see what we can do to a woman together. Completely overwhelm her with pleasure and make sure she's never going to leave unsatisfied. That she'd never need to find someone else to make her happy."

Somehow it made her feel better to know big, tough Lorenzo had his own weakness. Just like she seemed to have one for Trent and him and Owen. They reminded her of Moose, in a way, when she'd discovered him lost and wandering their neighborhood. They needed shelter, someone to show them how incredible they were, and suddenly she wanted to be that person.

"So what do you think about me? About how I'm hooking up with Trent for these three months, I mean?" Holly cleared her throat, hoping he couldn't tell how much this part pained her. "It's not so different from bringing someone home to share for a night. It's short-term. Our relationship has an expiration date. Why shouldn't we have some fun while I'm here?"

Whether *we* meant her and Trent or her and Lorenzo or her with all three of the roommates, she didn't specify. Because while she'd originally meant Trent, now she was wondering if Andi and Kari hadn't been right. They were grown-ass men and women with a mutual understanding.

Trent had explicitly given her the green light…

"I have to be honest." He looked down at her, shaking his head slightly as he did. "You kind of scare me. You're different and you mean something to Trent. Something more than just this inheritance bullshit."

"Me?" She snorted. "I don't think so. Otherwise he wouldn't have bolted from dinner the moment my mom implied we had some kind of personal connection."

"Ah, yeah. That's *exactly* why he bailed." Lorenzo huffed. "Because she's right. Why else would he be keeping you to himself? That's not how we operate."

Holly blinked. "Well, I mean technically he hasn't. Not entirely."

Both of them glanced over to the chairs he and Owen had occupied while they'd watched her and Trent like it was the world's most riveting spectator sport.

"Trust me. Nothing has been our same twisted sort of

normal since you got here." He looked away, and though he didn't say it, she could feel his hurt radiating off of him.

Oh hell no. She wasn't about to wound him like that woman who'd left him standing alone, ready to declare his love yet not receiving hers in return. He was a decent person. She'd seen him leap into action to help Trent when his father had passed away, and every day since.

"Lorenzo," she murmured as she reached up and laid her hand on his cheek, directing his gaze back to hers. He licked his lips and he stared at her mouth instead.

"I'm not trying to seduce you. I'm asking you to give Trent a chance." Lorenzo sighed. "He might have fucked up tonight, and I'm sure he will again. But he'll fix this once he's calmed down, I know he will. Give him another shot, okay? Please, *xuxu*."

"Do you want me to forgive him because you're a good friend or because you're hoping for side benefits? Something that involves more than jerking off while you're watching me come around your best friend?" Holly didn't shy away from what she really needed to know before she decided whether or not to try to fan the sparks flying between them into a full on flame.

"I'm not nearly as good a person as Trent, don't push me." He shifted, setting her slightly away from him, though he didn't let go of her shoulders. His hands were bigger than Trent's and a little softer too. He didn't have calluses from wrenching away on something in the shop.

Hell, he probably pampered himself more than she did, slathering oil on his shaved skin to appeal to his clientele. If she was still around the next time he was working, she was going to ask Trent to take her to his show. She wanted to see what she had been missing out on.

Unless he would give her a private demonstration...

"What if I want you too?" She ran her hand upward, across his chest. "What if I keep waking Trent up in the middle of the night to have sex with me after having dreams about you and Owen fucking me while Trent watches next? What if I want to visit your world as much as I wish Trent belonged in mine?"

"Does this answer the question for you?" Lorenzo, breathing hard, descended, crushing his lips against hers.

His kiss was wild and passionate, so different from Trent's methodical takeover of her senses. He stormed her, unleashing all of his pent-up desire and the ragged emotions he kept locked inside most of the time.

Yes, that's what she wanted from him. To make him take a risk and be as vulnerable as she felt.

Except that's when the front door opened and someone came in.

Trent! What would he think of busting them making out?

She wouldn't know, because instead it was Owen who strolled over, a shit-eating grin on his face. "Looks like I got home just in time."

15

Holly flashed back to dinner, when Trent had proclaimed to her mom that he wasn't a saint. Apparently she wasn't either. In fact, she was about to trade her halo for horns and never look back. Because everything in her was ready to take Owen up on the offer gleaming in his eyes.

Maybe it was because he and Lorenzo were reassuring the part of her that had felt betrayed by Trent walking out on her, unsure of her place in his life or of whether he was starting to think of her the way she was of him. Or maybe it was simply because she had some kind of connection with them.

Lorenzo was easy to justify. She'd felt something for him—a blend of empathy, attraction, and the need to rescue him after he'd been trampled on—like she had for Trent.

But Owen? She knew practically nothing about him other than that he was loyal, that he'd been gracious to her as she'd crashed into their lives, and that both Trent and Lorenzo saw him as an equal partner in their friendship and…more.

That was enough.

It made what she was doing seem even more wild, dangerous even. Like having sex with a stranger, yet with a safety net.

For once, being a little reckless appealed. Escaping from the regimented life she'd built for herself felt incredible. If she could be someone else for an hour or two, then maybe she could get through the next few months and go back to her duties as a caretaker without the despair or resentment that had been brewing within her for a while.

Lorenzo cradled her, murmuring things in Portuguese that she didn't understand yet still comprehended. He was reassuring, steady, and sure to keep her grounded when she finally let go of all rational thought so she could simply feel good.

Owen stalked closer, then sat on her opposite side. Sandwiched between them, an instant wave of comfort blended with desire came over her. They were going to take care of her. Make sure every hint of sadness and worry were blanked out by what they were about to do.

"Where's your husband?" Owen asked, looking toward Trent's room.

"He lost it." Lorenzo shook his head. "He'll be back. Why don't we show him why he should stick around next time instead of walking out on Holly?"

"My pleasure." Owen took her hand and squeezed. "I'm sorry, sweetheart. He's doing his best. And so are we. I hope this is the right thing, but if it's not, we'll take the fall. I swear."

And just like that, he'd made up her mind for her.

Holly craned her neck and met Owen halfway. He didn't mess around. It was like he'd stored up his emotions and they burst free at once in a shockwave of rapture. He cupped her face in his hands and kissed her so thoroughly that he took her breath away.

The massage of Lorenzo's hands across her back, supporting her and pushing her toward his best friend, only added to the thrill she got from Owen's mouth on hers. And when Lorenzo began to drag his lips across the crook of her neck, she thought she might come on the spot.

He chuckled, then added the barest hint of his teeth as his hands shifted, gliding down her ribs, his fingers grazing the sides of her breasts until he cupped her hips and his thumbs wandered onto the top swells of her ass.

Owen caught her sighs and the moan that slipped from between her parted lips, taking the opportunity to venture inside and tease her with his tongue. And when he needed a second, his breathing harsh and his eyes dilated, he let Lorenzo take a turn.

The contrast of his suave, almost elegant kisses compared to the rawness of Owen's was a potent aphrodisiac.

Owen trailed his fingers down her neck then between her breasts, over her shirt, making her shiver. "If Trent keeps insisting this is only a practical arrangement, without attachment, then I don't see why we shouldn't take him up on his assertion that we should explore, do whatever feels right."

His reasoning sounded so much like Trent's that it both reassured her and also disappointed her. That must have been what Trent had been trying to communicate when he'd given her permission to do...well, exactly this.

Same as he'd apparently told his friends. So why the hell should she restrict herself, as if she was putting her sex life on some kind of starvation diet?

You can only sleep with one man at a time, even if you're not really exclusive or, for that matter, married. Nope, there were no rules. No limits. No constraints. Her moral compass was freewheeling, trying to bend itself to a whole new set of rules than she'd considered before.

So she surrendered to her instincts and did what felt natural.

She reached for Owen and let Lorenzo support her as she arched her back and angled her face up to receive his next kiss. Whereas the first one she'd had with Trent had been sweet, and the one she'd shared with Lorenzo earlier had been passionate, making out with Owen was like a revolution.

His hand skimmed the bottom of her shirt before slipping beneath it and wandering upward until he could cup her breast. He squeezed as he kissed her. His fingers dipped beneath the lace edge of the cup the next time he let Lorenzo take his turn.

As she sucked on Lorenzo's tongue, which had invaded her mouth, she realized he'd slid his hand into her pants and was fondling her ass like Owen was doing to her breast.

Exactly how far was she going to let things go?

Was she going to have sex with them right there in the same spot Trent had fucked her while they watched? Maybe her husband would be the one to come home while they were otherwise engaged this time. Would he regret running out on her then, knowing he could have joined them if he'd been there with her? Or would he pass them by, go into his bedroom, and leave her to his best friends?

Somehow she didn't think he would do that.

It would destroy her if Trent was able to walk away when she was all in.

A sound in the background pulled her from the sensual haze they were enveloping her in.

And when it repeated, she groaned. She'd forgotten to text her mother when she'd arrived. Mom was probably going bananas. Or worse... Maybe something had happened.

"Wait, that's my phone. It's my mom's ringtone." Holly rummaged around blindly in the couch, looking for her purse. Owen found it first and handed it to her. Her mom never called her, preferring for Holly to reach out when it was convenient. It must be an emergency.

She fished in her bag for her phone. The instant her hand landed on the device, she was answering. "Mom? Are you okay?"

"I—" Her mother started bawling. Holly had only ever seen the woman cry at funerals and when Holly had graduated from college.

"Oh no, what's wrong?" Holly bolted to her feet, already searching for her shoes.

Lorenzo and Owen were right there with her, desire instantly replaced by concern on their handsome faces. They weren't pissed, but ready to spring into action with her. For the first time in forever, Holly felt like she had a support system in addition to being one for her mother.

If she wasn't so damn scared, she would have kissed them all over again.

"Nothing. Nothing." Her mother laughed and cried at

the same time. "It's my turn. I got the call. They have a kidney for me."

Then she sobbed along with her mother.

Owen raced to her side and gathered her close, his strong arms sheltering her even though he didn't know from what. Lorenzo was right there, too, bookending her and surrounding her with their protection even in Trent's absence.

"The aide is outside waiting for our cab." A tiny sliver of uncertainty slipped into her mother's tone. "We have to hurry. It's already being transported."

"I'll meet you at the hospital," Holly promised. "Everything is going to be fine. Better than fine. Congratulations, Mom. I'm so happy for you. I'll see you in a few minutes, okay?"

"I love you, Holly." Her mother added, "Bring Trent with you. You might need him."

"Yes, Mom. I'll bring...um...someone." She flashed a wobbly smile through her happy, and anxious, tears at Trent's best friends. They beamed down at her before squeezing her tight, obviously having realized what was about to happen.

"*Someones*," Lorenzo told her before putting his boots on while Owen opened his rideshare app and flagged the nearest driver.

This was really happening. Because of Trent.

She owed him everything, and as soon as he pulled his head out of his ass and resurfaced, she was going to make him see that they were too good of a match to throw things away because of their hang-ups.

In the meantime, Lorenzo took her hand in his and refused to let go while Owen made all the arrangements. Even if Trent wasn't there, he had ensured she was taken care of, and another piece of the puzzle fell into place for Holly.

This was what it was like to be in a relationship with more than one man.

She could see why her friends liked it so much, and not only for the spectacular sex. Someday, hopefully soon, she was going to find out what that aspect of living in a ménage was like.

Until then, she clung to Lorenzo, grateful to be sandwiched between him and Owen on the ride to hospital when her nerves kicked in and she started ruminating on each of the not-so-great things that could happen while chasing a better life, for herself, sure...but mostly for her mom.

The next few hours were going to change her life forever, but the past few had been doozies too.

16

———

Trent raced through the hospital doors, past the desk where he'd so recently received some of the worst news of his life, and all he could think about was Holly. Shit! He'd left her alone and look what had happened. He hadn't been there when she needed him after she'd done nothing but stick by his side.

Good thing he wasn't really her husband, because apparently he sucked at relationship shit.

He checked his phone and the text Owen had sent with Mrs. Hendricks' room number before flying along the ugly florescent-lit hallways until he burst into her ward. Several doors down, he saw his roommate hovering outside an open door.

"Lorenzo," he called, trying to be quiet though his heart was pounding so hard he wasn't sure if he'd screamed to hear himself over it.

His friend turned and offered a wan smile before meeting him halfway. "Thank God you're here. Holly is a mess. She needs you."

Trent peered over Lorenzo's head through the open

door to where Owen kept watch on Holly and her mom like a guard dog. He held Holly's hand as she clutched her mother's. The woman seemed frailer wrapped in the pale blue hospital gown as she lay in the robo-bed.

"She seems fine. Thanks to you two." He couldn't believe he'd taken off on her like that. He would understand if she was pissed. If she sent him away instead of dealing with his bullshit when she needed to focus on her mother's health.

Hell, it wouldn't be the first time someone he loved turned him away in their darkest hour.

"Um, this isn't the right place to hash things out but, just so there are no surprises, things kind of heated up with her right before we got the call." Lorenzo cleared his throat, looking guilty as fuck. "She was bummed about you bailing on dinner and I tried to console her, and next thing I knew..."

Trent's brows rose. "Really?"

"We made out with her, nothing more." Lorenzo held his hands up.

"Owen too?" Trent's mind raced, cataloging the possibilities. If Holly was open to more experimentation, or was starting to form a bond with his best friends, there could be a chance he wouldn't have to give her up after all. What if their fling truly could become something real?

"Sorry, Trent. We should have talked about how to take the next step." Lorenzo pinched the bridge of his nose. "It's just that she's so damn hot, and funny, and she was looking so sad and unsure..."

"Hey, it's not a problem." Trent put his hand on Lorenzo's shoulder and squeezed. "I told all three of you to do it if you felt like it. I meant that. So I guess she must think you're not half bad either."

"You think so?" Lorenzo's eyes turned molten gold.

Just then Holly noticed him in the hall. "Trent!"

He turned in time to see her mother wiggling her fingers in a weak wave toward him, and then Holly was running, throwing herself into his arms. He hugged her tight. "Hey. I'm so sorry I wasn't there when you got the call. How is your mom? How are you?"

She clung to him, trembling, before looking up with a sniffle. "She's perfect. I'm a disaster."

Trent ran his hand down her hair, loving the silky smoothness against his palm. It felt so nice he did it a few more times, until she went pliant against him. "Well, let's go sit with her until they take her to the OR, okay?"

"You don't mind, really?"

"Of course, not." He could finally breathe again when she leaned up against him, like she trusted him, and like whatever between them was about more than convenience or cash.

He wanted to believe it could be possible.

So he lifted her, loving how her legs wrapped automatically around his waist, and carried her into her mother's hospital room, where he took a seat in the single guest chair, the back of which aligned with the top of the bed. Holly ended up in his lap, facing her mom.

"Hello again, Mrs. Hendricks."

"Hey, yourself." She beamed at them, as if the sight of them back together was even more exciting than the kidney that could be the end to her suffering. "I'm glad you manned up enough to see that Holly needs you, even if you're afraid of what's between you."

He laughed. "Sorry, was it that obvious?"

Holly's mom nodded. "I didn't mean to frighten you

earlier. You're welcome to dinner or to visit anytime. And that has nothing to do with this."

She waved her hand weakly over herself lying in the hospital bed. "I'd be proud to have a son like you. Don't let anyone make you feel like you're not good enough to love someone or...many people."

Holly's mom's gaze shifted to Owen and Lorenzo, who were pacing nervously outside the door, tossing glances at him and Holly periodically.

"Oh, um..." Trent tried to think of some excuse or other, but his mind was too fried from having believed he'd blown things with Holly, or worse, that he didn't deserve her in the first place. Mrs. Hendricks knew about Andi and Kari and their relationships. She must. Holly lived with her and didn't seem like the type to keep secrets.

Hell, she'd even told her mother about their arrangement, which he was coming to hate.

Why couldn't he have kept his mouth closed and done as his father had wanted back in college? At least long enough to tap into his trust fund the old fashioned way. Then he could have given Holly and her mother the cash, no strings attached, before seeing where things went naturally between the four of them.

Had he doomed the one thing he now craved most for the dream he'd thought was his greatest desire? That would be just his luck.

"I might be sick, but I'm not blind," Mrs. Hendricks said, making her daughter sigh and rest her head on Trent's shoulder. "And I like what I see. So please, all of you, hold it together. No matter what happens tonight, you did everything possible to make the outcome positive for me. I love you for giving me this chance. Thank you."

Holly, Trent, and her mother were wiping tears from their cheeks when the doctor entered the room. Trent rocked Holly as they discussed the details of the surgery along with the long list of risks that came along with it. Holly went ashen as her mother signed off on page after page of informed consent documents.

The doctor said to Mrs. Hendricks then, "Okay, we're set. We're going to get you fixed up as best we can. It's going to be a long road after surgery, here in the hospital and then in rehab after, but I feel confident your chances are good. It looks like you have a lot to fight for." He smiled as he looked at Trent and Holly, huddled together.

Mrs. Hendricks nodded. "Yes, I do."

But Holly had gone stiff at the mention of rehab and how much time her mother would need to spend getting additional treatment. Had she included those expenses in the number she'd given him the night they'd gotten married?

It wasn't the time to discuss such trivial matters. Not when her mother's life hung in the balance. But Trent made a mental note to talk to Ford about getting a quote for the additional care the next time he touched base with the guy about the trust fund settlement.

Holly was brave as fuck when they came to get her mother, exchanging I-love-you's that—somehow—he got included in. It was only after nurses wheeled her out and the four of them sat in the cold, empty room that she broke down completely.

Trent rocked Holly, letting his T-shirt absorb her tears, and promised her everything would be okay even though he wasn't sure if he was telling the truth.

Even if her mother came through surgery and exceeded the doctor's expectations, he still didn't know how he was going to proceed with their sham marriage now that it was beginning to feel entirely too real.

And what would happen with Lorenzo and Owen when they went home together?

For the first time in his adult life, he felt jealous of his best friends and the fact that they'd fooled around with Holly when he wasn't there. It pissed him off because he'd thought he knew what he wanted, and now he was floundering when it mattered most.

He couldn't afford to screw this up.

Mostly, he was kicking himself for running away from their problems, even momentarily. Look what it had cost him. Maybe if he'd been there, things would have progressed...

He wasn't going to make that mistake again.

Trent clung to Holly for the entire seven hours her mother was in surgery, glad for the excuse to hold her close to his heart.

17

———

Holly should be worn out. She should be mentally and physically exhausted. Hell, she probably was underneath the adrenaline propelling her onward, but as she, Trent, Owen, and Lorenzo streamed into their house, she was wired.

"Is it crazy that I feel like going out dancing or something right now?" she asked to no one in particular as Moose barreled over to his humans and welcomed them home, her included. She laughed as he pranced around her feet licking her arm until she gave him the attention he sought.

"Yes," Lorenzo responded, though he paired his jab with a kind smile.

Trent put an arm around her and drew her to him, laying a loud, smacking kiss on her cheek. "You did so well tonight and so did your mom. After the doctor's post-surgery update and his incredible prognosis for her, it's no wonder you feel like you're on top of the world. You did it, Holly. You made the impossible happen."

She turned toward him, looping her arms around his neck. "No, Trent. *You* did. Thank you."

Holly practically climbed him right there in the entryway. She needed an outlet for the energy and relief pumping through her. What better way than by making his night after he'd made hers?

Besides, she still had to show him that shying away from whatever this was between them—as well as Owen and Lorenzo—wasn't the answer. He had to see that they were a great match, the four of them, as she had clearly realized during the long night they'd stayed glued to her side.

If it was only about sex or something base, they wouldn't have held her hand so tight while they waited for news. They wouldn't have brought her endless cups of coffee or given her a back rub when they realized her muscles were practically one giant cramp. This was something more, though she wasn't about to deny the physical attraction between them any longer.

She whispered in Trent's ear, "I want to pay you back for everything you've done. I want to give you what we both want."

He looked up at her with disbelief etched in his blue eyes, as if he was afraid to assume she was referring to a scorching night in bed. But really, how foolish would she be to turn down the opportunity to see what it was like to be the center of attention, caught between three magnificent men who made her feel entirely too much?

She nodded with a crooked grin, not exactly a seductress for all her willingness to try new things. "Yeah, that's what I'm talking about."

Holly didn't have to elaborate. Fortunately, Trent knew exactly what to do when she didn't. She squeaked when he spun her around a few times before marching toward his room. "Lorenzo. Owen. Let's go."

The guys hooted as they followed not two steps behind. Without ceremony, they began to strip, making Holly's mind flash freeze. Yeah, Lorenzo did it for a living, and if she had a fistful of dollars she'd be stuffing them into his underwear, right before he peeled them down his svelte hips.

"We might not have as much style, but we get just as naked," Owen teased as she ogled Lorenzo's tan skin dotted with dark hair.

Trent laughed at that. "Seriously, dude. Do you have to show off every damn time?"

The reminder that while she was brand new at this, they had done it many times with many women before, kind of rankled. So Holly shoved the thought aside. It vanished entirely when they turned toward her and began to remove her clothes for her.

Someone pulled her sweater over her head, as someone else walked her jeans down her hips. Then skilled hands unfastened her bra as her socks and then her panties were swiped from her body.

Faster than she could have done it herself, she was nude before them.

"Damn, Trent. I see why you've been keeping her to yourself." Lorenzo whistled as he took in her breasts and ass. She wasn't anything special, but he seemed to like what he saw. His cock thickened and he licked his lips. There was nothing coy or uncertain about their trajectory.

They were on the express train to Ménageville.

After the night they'd had, full of waiting that had damn near stopped her heart once or twice, that was perfectly all right with her. She needed them to make her feel alive right then. No excuses and no uncertainty.

Together they piled into Trent's oversized bed, which suddenly seemed precisely the right size. Trent sat, with his back braced against the tufted leather headboard, and situated her half on his lap, half between his thighs. When he grabbed her ankles and used them to position her legs, draped over his, then spread them wide, she let her head loll back on his shoulder.

Lorenzo and Owen crawled toward her, their stares glued to her exposed pussy.

"Who wants the first taste?" Trent asked. "She's sweet and makes the cutest sounds when she comes on your face."

"I do not—" There was no use in denying it. They were going to find out for themselves soon enough. Because before she could so much as finish her thought, Lorenzo had lunged ahead of Owen and began kissing his way up from her knee, straight to her clit.

Holly gasped when he began to lick her. Her hand automatically dropped to his head, twining in his long, thick hair. She used the grip to direct him so that whatever the hell he was doing with his tongue was the most effective. Incredibly effective.

Only Trent's arm around her middle kept her from bucking off him. His hard cock wedged in the furrow of her ass, making her shiver and him groan.

"That's right, let him make you feel so good." Trent kissed her neck and murmured in her ear, "And if you want to, you can get Owen ready to do the same."

Holly blinked her eyes open, realizing Owen had come up beside her hip. He was stroking his cock, getting it hard. She brushed his hand aside, replacing it with her own and using her grip to encourage him to rise.

When he did, his cock was at the right level for her to lean to the side and take him into her mouth, mimicking the motions Lorenzo was making on her own flesh with his tongue, and now his fingers too. When she gasped, Owen slid in even deeper. He might have choked her if Trent hadn't been paying such close attention. He moved her back, preventing her from gagging on Owen's long, thick shaft.

Sucking on his dick only made her crave having him, or one of the other guys, buried within her, easing the tension that was drawing her tighter and tighter from the inside out.

"Trent," she tried to call out, though it was garbled around Owen's cock. Owen groaned and caressed her face, telling her with his touch exactly how much she was pleasing him.

"You need more?" Trent asked.

Holly nodded, bobbing on Owen's cock, ridiculously pleased with herself when she tasted a spurt of his precome.

"Lorenzo, fuck her," Trent ordered.

His friend raised his head long enough to evaluate her expression. "Next time I'm going to make you come on my face. Trent wasn't lying. You taste so damn good I could do that all night."

"If you did, you'd drive her crazy." Trent hugged her, reassuring her they were going to give her everything she desired. "It's not enough, not by itself. Go ahead."

"I need to get some condoms." Lorenzo rolled to the side as if he was going to leave.

Holly tightened her grip on him. "No. You don't."

"She's on the pill and likes it when I come inside her." Trent explained when she couldn't find the words with her body aching.

"Son of a bitch," Owen rasped. "I've been tested recently, Holly. So has Lorenzo. You're good with that?"

"Yes, hurry." Holly writhed, trying to get closer to Lorenzo as he got to his knees between her and Trent's legs. But when he returned, this time with the blunt head of his cock instead of his fingers or his velvety tongue, her toes curled.

To know he was moments from being inside her, while Trent not only witnessed it but cheered them on, did something to her. She had never felt so ravenous or so bold and she loved being the person she'd always dreamed of being, if only for a few minutes.

Lorenzo guided his cock into her and used that incredible rolling motion of his hips to work his way inside with the smoothest strokes she'd ever experienced with a man. He was like a machine, if a very sophisticated one at that. He spread her apart, tunneling within her, the slickness of her channel inviting him deeper.

Holly sucked harder on Owen, glad for a task to focus on given the overwhelming sensations of being trapped between three sexy men. He cursed, then looked down at where Lorenzo was joined with her. "Shit, that's hot. Look at how well she takes you. Give it to her, Lorenzo. Make her come the first time."

First? Oh God, with three of them, she could probably have her fill. Or maybe more than she could handle, they'd have to see. What made her think she could satisfy three virile men at once?

Trent petted her stomach and played with her breasts.

"You're doing great, Holly. Don't worry. All you have to do is enjoy. That's what turns us on the most, okay?"

She nodded, thrilling Owen again. Lorenzo picked up the pace, alternating curses with what she assumed were terms of endearment as he rocked within her. Trent helped too by gliding his hand downward. He used his middle finger to rub circles on her clit, getting it trapped between her body and Lorenzo's as he ground against her. Her pussy hugged his cock, trying not to let it escape.

"Damn it. This is too good. I'm not going to be able to last." Lorenzo threw his head back, his mane of onyx hair making him look like he belonged on some sort of high-end shampoo commercial.

Holly dropped one hand to Trent's and squeezed, letting him know that she wasn't going to be able to resist Lorenzo's skilled maneuvers either.

In fact, she was already starting to quiver around him, the anxiety and anticipation of the evening transforming into something that demanded an outlet.

"She's with you," Trent promised Lorenzo. "She needs you as badly as you need her. Go ahead, Lorenzo. Come. Shoot deep inside her."

"Seriously?" Lorenzo's stride hitched at that. "You're sure? I've never done that before. Not with anyone."

Holly made a sound of undeniable assent. That was the best she could do when she was about to explode. Another few pumps and she was going to lose it all over Lorenzo.

"Go ahead, Lorenzo. Flood her pussy so Owen knows you've been there when he goes next." Trent pushed Holly right over the edge into orgasm with that filthy thought.

She shattered, wringing Lorenzo's cock and pulling him into his own climax.

He roared and bucked before the hot jets of his release washed over her pulsing flesh. He rode her through the spasms until Owen begged for mercy. "Hurry, Lorenzo. Her mouth is amazing too. I want to be in her when I come."

Lorenzo sighed as he pulled out of her, as if he never wanted to leave. And to be honest, she would have welcomed him longer if she didn't have to consider the needs of her other partners too. There would, hopefully, be plenty of other opportunities for them both.

"Hang on." Trent stopped Owen when he slipped from her mouth and traded places with Lorenzo. "She's probably going to need some help to come again quickly. Let me get under her."

The next thing Holly knew, her world was rotating. And when it stopped, she was on all fours, over Trent, who lay on his back beneath her. Except he'd turned around so that instead of being face to face, she was even with his cock.

He didn't have to explain his intention. She went down on him in a single deep stroke that made his ass clench and lifted him higher on the bed. In sweet retaliation, he latched his mouth onto her pussy and sucked. If he could taste Lorenzo on her, he didn't complain.

Distracted, she didn't realize that she was on full display for his friends until Owen grabbed her ass, spread her wide, then sank into her pussy. Lorenzo's seed made it easy for him to slide deep on the first stroke. His abdomen tapped her ass and helped her take more of Trent's cock in her mouth as he rode her.

Lorenzo lay down alongside them and ran his hands all over her from her back to her shoulders and even to what he could reach of her breasts. He told her over and over how gorgeous she was and how thoroughly she had pleased him. When she needed a break, and slid Trent's cock from between her lips to stroke him with her hand, Lorenzo angled her head toward himself and treated her to another of his sensual kisses.

That's when she stiffened.

The combination of Trent's eating, Owen's fucking, and Lorenzo's kissing was impossible to withstand. She bit his lip in warning.

Lorenzo chuckled as he called out to his friends, "Get ready, Owen. She's going to lose it any second."

"I can feel her. She's clamping down on my cock. Fuck. So damn tight." His next strokes were harder and less sophisticated than Lorenzo's. The rough edge was exactly what Holly needed to trigger her explosion. She shuddered as she unraveled, thankful for Trent, Lorenzo, and Owen supporting her as she lost herself to the moment.

Owen roared, then unloaded inside her, the heat of his come warming her from within.

Trent wasn't as patient as Lorenzo had been, or maybe he'd reached his limit. The instant Owen had finished releasing inside her, he rolled her to her back, dislodging his friend and blanketing her with his body.

Lorenzo was still on one side of them and Owen joined them on the other, stretched out full length alongside her. Owen, Trent, and Lorenzo took turns kissing her, their frantic pace slowing as the initial blaze turned into something deeper and longer lasting.

Now that she'd come twice, they'd taken the edge off her desire.

Trent began to fuck her, with a steady, unrelenting force that was going to rock her entire world. Hell, it already had. While one of his friends feasted on her lips, he said, "Holly, you're perfect. I swear, you were made for this, just like we were."

She arched, fitting herself to him as tightly as she could, because she desperately wanted to believe it was true and that they had been destined for each other. They certainly seemed to mesh well.

He looked straight into her eyes and smiled as he bottomed out in her pussy. The wet noise his motions made only reminded them both that his friends had been there before him. That they'd given her more pleasure than she'd experienced in a single night before.

Trent called her name, over and over as he rocked into her. Finally she realized that this time it was him who needed encouragement. Reassurance. And maybe...hope.

She twisted her head until her lips were free of Owen's, then said, "Yes, Trent. It feels right when you're inside me. When we're together like this. Maybe it was meant to be. I've never felt something as amazing as what we've done tonight and if you don't stop fucking me like that...just like that...I'm going to come again. With you."

Trent's stare locked on hers. He cursed, then repeated the same motion with incredible precision. "Yes, Holly. Please, share this with me. Please."

She reached up and wrapped her arms around him, holding him close as they flew together, the cheers of his best friends pushing them higher and making the ride last longer.

He pumped into her, overflowing her with the proof of how intensely their exchange moved him.

And when he might have crushed her, completely spent, Lorenzo brought him down to the side, still joined with her. It was dead silent, none of them wanting to ruin the moment, which seemed nearly sacred to her.

Holly floated on the euphoria they'd gifted her with, soaking in every last drop of bliss.

It seemed they did the same, as the only sounds were Trent's labored breaths and the whisper of their hands over her skin as they brought her gently back to reality.

One where they weren't hers to keep, but only to play with for a while. And suddenly that seemed like it could never be enough.

Oh shit, what had she done?

18

———

Trent groaned as every muscle in his body liquefied. He had never come so hard or so often as he had lately. And that was the problem. He was getting too damn used to Holly and how amazing it was to have her in both his bed and his life.

She sighed and curled up against him, utterly relaxed and trusting.

He played with her hair as Lorenzo and Owen ran their hands over her, as if they couldn't stop touching her for a moment now that they had permission to do so. He didn't blame them. Holly was the most beautiful, most amazing woman he'd ever had the pleasure to fuck or even to know.

And that's why he couldn't stand the thought of her leaving in a few short months. Not after he had adjusted to having her nearby. After what they'd done that night, it would be impossible to say goodbye and watch her walk away for good.

Finally having vented her fear and euphoria from the hospital, turning it into ecstasy and sexual energy that had nearly burned them all alive, she seemed to shrink. With a sniffle she murmured, "Eight weeks in the hospital and rehab. How much do you think that's going to cost?"

"I was thinking about that..." Trent cleared his throat, hoping she wouldn't see through him. But she'd given him the perfect opening. "Our partnership is working out so well. Why don't we extend it?"

Her face lit up. "You don't want to call it quits after ninety days anymore?"

Lorenzo and Owen fist bumped over them.

"No." He smiled as he shook his head. "If you'll agree to stay, say, another three months? I'd be glad to pay for your mother's rehab and her hospital expenses."

"Oh." Holly's face fell and she crawled over him to get out of bed.

That hadn't been the reaction he'd been expecting.

Owen punched him in the shoulder.

"Ow, what? What did I say?" Trent looked between Holly's face, now devoid of her previous contentment and joy, to Lorenzo's glare and Owen's clenched jaw.

"You said you want to buy more time to fuck me." Holly threw her hands up. "When you promised me before that you weren't paying me for sex. If that's all this is to you, thanks but no fucking thanks."

She started gathering her clothes and putting them on so sharply he thought she might tear them in the process.

"Your mom *needs* that care." Trent tried again to make her see reason.

"Fuck you, she'll have it. Even if I have to get ten jobs to pay for it." Holly crossed her arms over her now fully clothed body. He missed the sight of her lush breasts and the soft pink skin of her stomach and thighs. "But I will not take another penny of your money so that you can convince yourself this is some sort of transaction and nothing more."

She whipped her head to the side, but it was too late; he'd seen the tears gathering in her gorgeous eyes. Shit, and now he'd hurt her, just like he'd been afraid of all along.

He wasn't cut out for a relationship. She was right to leave him before they fucked each other up completely.

Trent flopped onto his back and stared blankly at the ceiling.

"Let me walk you home, Holly," Lorenzo offered.

"No. I need time to myself. Without Trent, or any of you." She snatched her purse off the bedside table and jammed her feet into her shoes. "I have to think, and you screw with my head. All of you."

Trent didn't argue, sure that it was true. Hadn't his father always told him that the abomination of his sexuality would ruin any woman he tried to love that way?

"At least take Moose with you," Owen suggested.

"No. He'd be more likely to lick someone to death than to attack them, and I'm not sure when I'll be back. Because at the end of the day, or ninety days, it's my stupid heart that's going to be broken. I can already tell I'm falling for you."

His eyes cut to hers at that. She stared straight into Trent's soul, but he knew she had directed her statement at the three of them. "And that's the one thing I can't afford. None of us can. Especially not you, despite your spare millions."

Damn it!

"Holly, wait!" What the hell had she said? Did she feel like he did? That this was more than a fucking sham marriage they were living out? Had he ruined everything by refusing to admit it, even to himself, as she was obviously brave enough to do?

It was too late. She'd already gone, slamming the door behind her.

The sound reverberated through the house and his aching chest. Though he'd been preparing himself every minute they spent together for the moment he'd have to give her up again, he realized that nothing was going to keep him safe if they kept going like they were.

And that's why he didn't chase after her and beg for forgiveness, despite Lorenzo and Owen shouting at him to do exactly that.

19

Tears blurred Holly's vision as she jogged through the streets toward her mother's apartment. Sure, it was empty, but maybe that's what she needed. Some time alone to really think about the mistakes she was making and how bad the consequences would be if she didn't fix them now, before she couldn't repair the damage they would wreak.

Turn back from the dangerous, impulsive part of her that was rushing headlong into a one-sided relationship, despite the fact that it was with three separate people.

Upset and still mostly boneless from the endless orgasms Trent and his roommates had showered her with, she wasn't paying much attention to her surroundings. When the headlights of an oncoming car blasted her with blinding blue light, she realized she must have nearly run out in front of someone.

She held up her hands, casting dark shadows onto her face. "Sorry, sorry!"

But that only made the perfect grip for whoever it was that burst from the passenger side of the vehicle and snatched her up. She was stuffed halfway into the backseat before she even registered what was happening and began to thrash.

Screaming, she kicked, punched, and even bit who-knew-what part of the refrigerator-sized man squashing her into the vehicle and sitting beside her to keep her from escaping. He didn't give a shit that she knocked her head hard enough to see starbursts that reminded her of the fireworks the lawyers had arranged in Kari's honor when she'd agreed to be their wife.

Trent would probably shoot off similar ones the day they got divorced.

That thought shouldn't have hurt worse than the rough grip of whoever was assailing her, tying a blindfold around her face and cinching it tight enough that she thought her nose might be permanently misshapened.

"Don't make this harder than it has to be!" a second man, from the front seat, the driver she thought, kept yelling at her until his instructions finally penetrated her terror and despair. "We don't want to hurt you. Trent might not pay top dollar for damaged goods."

At Trent's name, she froze. This wasn't some random abduction. Oh, fuck.

"What—?" Her voice cracked. "What do you mean?"

"Behave yourself and you'll be fine. We're not going to hurt you. We want to sell you."

Tires squealed as she was slammed backward into the seat. Her assailants took off, whisking her away from the only people who might be able to help. Hell, no one else would even realize she was gone.

Neither would Trent, most likely. It wasn't like he was going to come after her and beg her to return. He'd gotten what he needed. *And* what he wanted.

"Sorry to tell you, I don't think I'm worth much." Okay, that probably wasn't the smartest thing she'd ever said. The money they were after was her only ticket out of this mess.

Think, Holly! She forced panic down and tried to devise a strategy that didn't involve crying and hoping for the best.

"Half of the money he's scamming from his family sounds more than fair to me." The man cackled and the motion churned the acid that had already been bubbling in her stomach.

Thirty-five million dollars? He didn't put even a fraction of that much value on her.

Come on, he'd flat out just told her that another three months of her life and spreading her legs for him and his friends were worth a few hundred thousand dollars max. What would he want for getting her out of this mess?

Trent had made it clear that he wasn't about to sacrifice reaching his goals for anything. He was in it for the money. And that meant she was doomed. She'd seen the financial plans for his company. He didn't have thirty-five mil of wiggle room in the budget and he'd shown her tonight that bringing his new technology to market was his only priority.

No way would he give it up for her or anyone else, and that meant she was screwed.

Hopefully, he'd feel bad enough about getting her killed that he'd take care of her mom. It was the least he could do, really.

Because when the guy beside her jammed something cold and metallic into her ribs, she just assumed it was a gun. And when he told her not to speak until they made it to wherever the hell they were taking her so they could make their demands, she figured she wasn't going to make it out of the situation alive.

The worst thing was, as she struggled against the zip tie one of his accomplices lashed her wrists with, she wished she'd kept her mouth shut earlier so that she could still be nestled—warm and cozy, satisfied—in Trent's bed, at the center of a man tangle composed of him, Lorenzo, and Owen. When she imagined their arms wrapped around her and their big bodies sheltering her from whatever these criminals were about to do to her, a sense of peace washed over her, even knowing she was telling herself the worst sort of fairy tale.

The kind with an unhappy ending.

Even if she managed to escape, she was still doomed to be broken. That was the problem with having an affair for money instead of for love.

For the conclusion of Holly, Trent, Owen, and Lorenzo's story, click HERE to read Four Love (Ever & Always Duet, Book 2).

Book Two of the
Ever & Always Duet
FOUR
LOVE
NEW YORK TIMES & USA TODAY BESTSELLING AUTHOR
JAYNE RYLON

Want to know more about Andi, Cooper, Reed, and Simon or Kari's billionaire boyfriends? You're in luck!

THE 4-EVER DUET (Andi)
4-Ever Mine
4-Ever Theirs

THE EVER AFTER DUET (Kari)
Fourplay
Fourkeeps

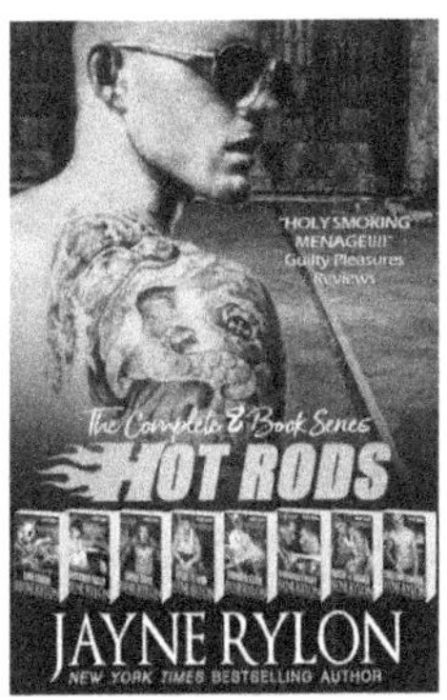

If you like steamy menage stories and missed out on the Powertools: Hot Rods series, you can buy all eight books in a discounted single-volume boxset by clicking HERE.

CLAIM A $5 GIFT CERTIFICATE

Jayne is so sure you will love her books, she'd like you to try any one of your choosing for free. Claim your $5 gift certificate by signing up for her newsletter. You'll also learn about freebies, new releases, extras, appearances, and more!

www.jaynerylon.com/newsletter

WHAT WAS YOUR FAVORITE PART?

Did you enjoy this book? If so, please leave a review and tell your friends about it. Word of mouth and online reviews are immensely helpful and greatly appreciated.

JAYNE'S SHOP

Check out Jayne's online shop for autographed print
books, direct download ebooks, reading-themed apparel
up to size 5XL, mugs, tote bags, notebooks, Mr. Rylon's
wood (you'll have to see it for yourself!) and more.
www.jaynerylon.com/shop

LISTEN UP!

The majority of Jayne's books are also available in audio format on Audible, Amazon and iTunes.

ABOUT THE AUTHOR

Jayne Rylon is a *New York Times* and *USA Today* bestselling author who has sold more than one million books. She has received numerous industry awards including the Romantic Times Reviewers' Choice Award for Best Indie Erotic Romance and the Swirl Award, which recognizes excellence in diverse romance. She is an Honor Roll member of the Romance Writers of America.

Jayne's stories used to begin as daydreams in seemingly endless business meetings, but now she is a full time author, who employs the skills she learned from her straight-laced corporate existence in the business of writing. She lives in Ohio with her husband, the infamous Mr. Rylon. When she can escape her purple office, she loves to travel the world, avoid speeding tickets in her beloved Sky, SCUBA dive, hunt Pokemon, and–of course–read.

Jayne Loves To Hear From Readers
www.jaynerylon.com
contact@jaynerylon.com
PO Box 10, Pickerington, OH 43147

facebook.com/jaynerylon

twitter.com/JayneRylon

instagram.com/jaynerylon

youtube.com/jaynerylonbooks

bookbub.com/profile/jayne-rylon

amazon.com/author/jaynerylon

ALSO BY JAYNE RYLON

4-EVER

A New Adult Reverse Harem Series

4-Ever Theirs

4-Ever Mine

EVER AFTER DUET

Reverse Harem Featuring Characters From The 4-Ever Series

Fourplay

Fourkeeps

EVER & ALWAYS DUET

Reverse Harem Featuring Characters from the 4-Ever and Ever After Duets

Four Money

Four Love

POWERTOOLS: THE ORIGINAL CREW

Five Guys Who Get It On With Each Other & One Girl. Enough Said?

Kate's Crew

Morgan's Surprise

Kayla's Gift

Devon's Pair

Nailed to the Wall

Hammer it Home

More the Merrier *NEW*

POWERTOOLS: HOT RODS

Powertools Spin Off. Keep up with the Crew plus...

Seven Guys & One Girl. Enough Said?

King Cobra

Mustang Sally

Super Nova

Rebel on the Run

Swinger Style

Barracuda's Heart

Touch of Amber

Long Time Coming

POWERTOOLS: HOT RIDES

Powertools and Hot Rods Spin Off.

Menage and Motorcycles

Wild Ride

Slow Ride

Hard Ride

Joy Ride

Rough Ride

POWERTOOLS: RETURN OF THE CREW

The original crew is back with more steamy menage stories!

Screwed

Drilled

Grind

Pound

MEN IN BLUE

Hot Cops Save Women In Danger

Night is Darkest

Razor's Edge

Mistress's Master

Spread Your Wings

Wounded Hearts

Bound For You

DIVEMASTERS

Sexy SCUBA Instructors By Day, Doms On A Mega-Yacht By Night

Going Down

Going Deep

Going Hard

STANDALONE

Menage

Middleman

Nice & Naughty

Contemporary

Where There's Smoke

Report For Booty

COMPASS BROTHERS

Modern Western Family Drama Plus Lots Of Steamy Sex

Northern Exposure

Southern Comfort

Eastern Ambitions

Western Ties

COMPASS GIRLS

Daughters Of The Compass Brothers Drive Their Dads Crazy And Fall In Love

Winter's Thaw

Hope Springs

Summer Fling

Falling Softly

COMPASS BOYS

Sons Of The Compass Brothers Fall In Love

Heaven on Earth

Into the Fire

Still Waters

Light as Air

PLAY DOCTOR

Naughty Sexual Psychology Experiments Anyone?

Dream Machine

Healing Touch

RED LIGHT

A Hooker Who Loves Her Job

Complete Red Light Series Boxset

FREE - Through My Window - FREE

Star

Can't Buy Love

Free For All

PICK YOUR PLEASURES

Choose Your Own Adventure Romances!

Pick Your Pleasure

Pick Your Pleasure 2

RACING FOR LOVE

MMF Menages With Race-Car Driver Heroes

Complete Series Boxset

Driven

Shifting Gears

PARANORMALS

Vampires, Witches, And A Man Trapped In A Painting

Paranormal Double Pack Boxset

Picture Perfect

Reborn

PENTHOUSE PLEASURES

Naughty Manhattanite Neighbors Find Kinky Love

Taboo

Kinky

Sinner

Mentor

ROAMING WITH THE RYLONS

Non-fiction Travelogues about Jayne & Mr. Rylon's Adventures

Australia and New Zealand

www.ingramcontent.com/pod-product-compliance
Lightning Source LLC
Chambersburg PA
CBHW070948190726
48292CB00004B/1382